The Smoke is Me, Burning

C A Blintzios

KERNPUNKT • PRESS

Copyright © 2022 by KERNPUNKT Press

All rights reserved. This book or any portion thereof may not be reproduced or used in any manner whatsoever without the express written permission of the publisher.

Cover Art: James Barker
Book Design: Jesi Buell
Editors: Patrick Parks and Jesi Buell

ISBN-13 978-1-7343065-2-1

KERNPUNKT Press
Hamilton, New York 13346

www.kernpunktpress.com

To Joey.

For everything seen, heard and kept.

Whoever is delighted in solitude, is either a wild beast or a god.
- Aristotle

Artwork by Ilia Strigari

I am not dead meat walking.

I know this because of the way a dancer made me feel. I know that watching him restored my chest with air and cleared the sulphur. He was alone on stage, for an hour–moving as if placed on a moon-lit seabed. His body was covered in ivory paint against a black background. Light bulbs hung from wires above his head like a halo, a motel sign, buzzing on and off. He pulled at thick ropes tied to his body. The ropes were attached to chairs and objects pulled slowly from the stage by invisible hands. He constricted himself to make them all stay and the lights above his head flickered in defiance. There was black dust spread over the floor that soiled his body as he danced, as he fought. By the end it was as if he had been pulled through coal. Painted, panther-black. A calm voice spoke through a gramophone's spout to the right–a woman's voice. It listed the Latin genus of every human ancestor–*Homo Habilis, Australopithecus Afarensis, Neanderthal*–as the dancer clung to his ropes, pulling and thrashing. Eggshell skin stained with ash. Muscle, knotted over bone.

By the end he sat cross-legged, rocking back and forth, his ropes limp. The voice receded. The light sank low. Slowly he looked up and out into the audience. Brought both palms up to his face. His arms dropped. He stared up at the last light bulb as it flickered and went out. From somewhere behind him in the dark came a rattling, as thousands of pinecones were emptied onto the stage and crashed into his body. He sat, taking every single collision until he was completely smothered. The last pinecone rolled off the stage, down between my feet. Part of me was that dancer pulled through ashes. The part that wasn't carrion, maggots and blowflies.

Courage. Courage I choose thee.

Part I.

Summers of Black Sunlight

THE BALD-KNOB

There are four legends concerning Prometheus. According to the second,

hounded by the pain of beaks tearing his body.

He pressed himself deeper and deeper into the rock.

Until he became one with it.

BLAKE

Everybody knows how to dress down a buck.

First you hang the body over a gut bucket. You cut the neck open so it grins. You let it drain for hours and then you take the front legs. You want a good knife. Flesh dulls the blade. Make two swift cuts through the sinew and then through the bones with a hacksaw – they should come right off. Then take the head. Cut and follow through with a hacksaw, until you touch the air on the other side. Blast it all with cold water and stop the meat crying. Take the knife and make a Y shape down middle of the sternum. Tear it from ass to neck, all the way. Then another line from the back limb into the central cut. Make two slits above the knees for handles. Pull down hard so that the skin falls off like a sweater. When the animal's young you need to tug a little harder. Afterwards you'll see all the maps hidden under the skin. Make the deepest cut across the horizon. It all needs to go. Pull down from the rib cage and it'll sound like a waterfall, it'll stop the meat crying.

In deer season our town emptied. The two main roads went still and silent. An occasional vehicle passed over the asphalt, shy as a coyote and its engine met with gunshots in the trees. All the men cleared out.

Left the women and children alone with the sounds of their stomachs. Left a buzzing in the mind. Men needed to feel like killers sometimes. Every house had antlers collecting dust. Crafted into hilts and handles for bush knives, crowns of thorns fixed to door frames. The dogs were manic in deer season. Foam frothed at their mouths and like oceans they dragged the world in behind them. Hunting is all men had after the crops went bad. Their wives, daughters, sisters and mothers liked it too. They liked having the smell of something wild hanging in the barn, strung up ready for peeling. Deer meat was good smoked—it got us through the winter.

Vern was electric then. His whole body changed shape. Maw said he was like a cobra. Shoulders rounded. Eyes all-pupil. There was a shadow that followed him around, a shadow the size of a small boy. It went everywhere with him, stood still in corners as he worked his herd. The boy only disappeared during deer season. My brother and I weren't allowed to go hunting with the men. I remember the silence now, how quiet our farm was, there were no cars, no birds in the sky. The air closed in like jaws. It was when all the men left and all the dogs left that we found Wilf Batty in the woods behind our home. It was during deer season that a child my age was dumped under the pines, hogtied, dressed out like a prize buck. The memory of finding him is an empty space that hums.

Wilf was slow. A loggerhead. There were some words he couldn't say right. He opened and closed his mouth without talking. He'd look you in the eyes and leave it too long before he blinked. Wilf Batty liked to screw things together that didn't fit, wrong things, like he was mak-ing friends for himself. Mismatched and misshapen— chimerical. One time he came to school with a dead wood pigeon under his arm. In front of everyone he twisted its head off and it crackled like bubble wrap. He tried to stitch it onto the body of a girl's doll with string and glue but it wobbled off and fell and some of us laughed at him. These new creatures were words to the loggerhead, they were his voice. The girl screamed and he was beaten badly in front of everyone with a long thin stick. They made Wilf crouch down low, put his arms under his legs and hop from one side of the yard to the other like a frog. His chin trembled and we could all see the whites of his eyes. Whenever he put his hands out to catch a fall, they smacked him across the back with a cane and turned his shirt salmon-pink. Wilf Batty got the cane too often.

I don't remember much beyond the pain in my left eye. After we found him, people whispered and averted their gazes. They talked about how there was a light rain bleeding through sunbeams on that morning – how it meant the Devil was beating his wife silly. All I remember is smoke, pluming from the fields.

Blue smoke, like the sea was on fire.

JAMIE

Jamie is running. Leaves crunch beneath his feet. Running through the mists of fall. Blake comes up behind, more timid, a baby deer. Silence, the breath rattles. He is alive in that fragment. Weaving stark between the thick pine. He roars, he squeals with the freedom of it. Stamps his feet into the soil. Grabs bunches of dead leaves—orange, red and brown and throws them up into a fountain of scales. Exalt, exalt, exalt. He is breathed in and out again by the wild. Nature is his mother. He picks up a snakeskin and makes it a whip. He thrashes away at branch-es with a long thin stick. Deeper and deeper, with fewer birds singing. Exalt, exalt, exalt.

Blake's words clatter behind him like old pots and pans. He calls out over and over again but Jamie doesn't care. He is running now. Running into the clearing where nothing grows. In this pinched space he halts. He sees. Mangled and white like a petal. The child hangs, inches off the ground swinging ever so slightly. A branch creaks above his body. Hands and feet all tied together like flowers. Gravity bleeds him out. The slow boy swings back and forth, dressed, sliced in all the right places.

Jamie steps up closer. This is the death of a god. A lotus blooms in his chest. The only birds here are buzzards. Two of them lope sheepishly like drunk old men. They fly up and fall back down. No grip in their toes. They jab until a small wound unravels. Jamie yells and waves the stick over his head, making himself large. They fall back flapping and hissing, then return. Jamie is under the child now, stick raised, protecting him from carrion birds. The rope twists and sings. Blake's voice swells through the undergrowth and somewhere a possum grins.

Sunlight splinters through the trees and gathers into a pool of light beneath the swinging child. Into the soil like a buried mirror. Then Jamie sees it. A little further out, almost invisible—but there. Stick in one hand, snakeskin in the other. That which stares back and lives in the trees of the mind. Branches crack, low hoots and high-pitched yelps. Shoulders, boots, breath in the ears. Antlers, musk and so many masks. Blake's scream swings him back around and the stick leaves Jamie's hand. His brother is silent, stiffened in shock, whimpering. The buzzards beat their wings into the ground. Jamie holds Blake close as everything moves in to devour the swinging child.

THE BALD-KNOB

There are people in places that have struck deals with the spirit world. They fill banana skins with rice and take them to the edge of their village. Place them next to each other in a circle. Little by little grains of rice topple from the skins. Some see ghosts doing this, others see ants working. They take the offering and leave the villagers be. They know that one world shouldn't spill over into another. Arkansas is a creation state, a finishing-up state. Nature intended it for a hunting ground.

BLAKE

When I was five years old my little brother threw a stick into my left eye. Like a javelin, it blinded me. I had been teasing him, telling him that when he ran his legs dangled like a chicken's. Chicken Legs, the name stuck from that day on. I don't know why I did this; I felt the words spill from my mouth but didn't recognize the voice as mine. We were playing in the woods behind our house where the Howlers lived. No one remembered what they looked like, but the howls remained, the whistling. The grass always moved.

My brother was eighteen months younger than me. We called him the monkey, the wildcat. He pulled my toys apart. My little green army men. I let him have the release and watched heads and limbs pile up on the bedroom floor like a Mayan ceremony. I could always snap them back into place if I wanted. The fury inside my brother couldn't be contained in the everyday way of things, he needed to push into a crack in the glass, to dig until he found the warm heart of earthworms and pick at a scab until it bled and he could see the pink beneath, winking.

Pines, firs and conifers loomed large beyond the chicken wire fence of our backyard. Over where we weren't supposed to be. With the gods and their clicking tongues and their leathery fingers. The unkilled, uncaught, forever flourishing monsters. In the middle of the fall, I was blinded. Beneath canopies, between sunbeams that made yolk on the forest floor. When I think back, it's as if I'm floating above it, outside of my body, hovering. I feel that the Howlers watched us in the same way, from their canopies. Hands twisting the bark until it creaked. I believe that they watched me lose my sight.

I can still see him running. A pile of red and brown leaves clutched to his chest. He swivels his head back to see where I am. I follow the me that follows him. I watch as he falls over a tree root, snot stuck thick between nose and mouth, frozen solid. I hear him pant like a dog as he picks himself up, mud over the knees. Breath fluttering like water sprinklers. I never felt good in the pinewood. The wilderness had a heart of caterpillar nests, needles and the skeletons of small birds. All hidden, all deep. It would burst someday and grow over everything. The way weeds grew through and constricted old cars. The woods cir-cled us, even when we were at home in our beds. From one moment to the next we could be gone without a trace, grown over – gulped down. Our bones made into xylophones, our skulls hollowed out and turned upside down for drinking goblets.

Jamie didn't feel these things. He liked to run around pre-tending he was invisible and watch me scramble around like a fool in the dark. He liked his lungs fit to explode and was deaf to me when I said that the soil was uncoiling ready to drag us under, that things with wings were stretching out in the branches ready to pluck us off the ground. Ready to carry us away into the mountain caves. They were everywhere, counting our little breaths like coins. Making the bark creak. By then my concept of death was concrete. Death was the bodies of our six dogs. Death was what looking at them *felt* like. Before the age of five I'd seen most of them poisoned, drowned, or run over. Maw never let us name the animals; they were just dogs. They hadn't all died at once, but close enough to where I could see them all in a line, tongues hanging out. Mongrels and bastards, pups found by the as-phalt. Crying inside boxes. Old mutts that no one wanted. We always needed protectors.

My childhood was spent searching for the sad flame in a dog's eyes. All of them looked up with the same desperation. They flocked like pigeons to breadcrumbs when our mother threw scraps and soup bones into the yard. Seeing them all die made me believe in the Devil. Made me believe that he was everything I didn't understand. I looked for signs from the universe to protect me from joining them, from becoming another body with its tongue hanging out. Jamie bent to pick a snakeskin off the ground with his thumb and forefinger, the woods were known for their vipers. He examined its translucence in the light with cotton-wool focus. His eyes darted up and with a smirk he exploded flailing the thing around like a whip, squealing with electricity. A ball of bile rolled up into my throat. The bark creaked a little harder. The day Jamie blinded me, my skin felt like it was crawling with insects.

I watched him run sprite-like, almost ceremonial. His body bent over the steaming soil. Knees close to his face, jerking his head back into the sky. He turned and flung the skin at me like a slingshot, catching it with the pressure of his thumb. If he let go, it would've hit me full in the face. That snakeskin was a used condom, diaphanous and slime-filled, someone else's business. Later I found out that the acres of woodland behind our house were used for more than just child's play.

Beer cans, pipes, syringes and clothes were scattered like remnants of an encampment. Other things were hidden there too. All the secrets of our small town fossilized in the sap of those pines, like mosquitoes.

The memory hardens. Like before a glacier slips into seawater. My jaw opened on its hinge. He watched me, head tilted, condom hanging low, brushing the tips of leaves on the ground. He stopped running and his face creased up as he took me in with the fiery silence of a bull. I don't believe that I was present in that moment. I was muted and made to watch things exiled up on some high crag. Constricted, voiceless. Jamie threw the stick he'd been swinging around as a sword. He needed to put the animal down. The weapon entered my body. Drapes closed on my thoughts—a sand-filled heaviness, feet crushing fruit. Distortion bounced off of every tree-trunk like laughter. Through the split I felt something broken, black and inky, pass into me. I felt a new life push its way into existence. I tugged the twig out. With trembling finger tips, I let it drop onto leaves and soil. The panic was peripheral, like wolves watching sheep.

I lay down on my back and earth fused into my body. Large breaths flooded my sinuses. I worried about being dragged under. Through locked fingers a bone-white sky shivered. Branches slithered, blood. I don't know how long I waited. Jamie dragged me by my feet. All the way back to the tree line, screaming his lungs dry. I was his brother again. Maw told me later that the whole thing was butchery. Vern drove us to the hospital miles out. His pickup shook over the road like a mouth full of loose teeth. Maw held my head against her chest. I pictured her heart, her lungs like plastic bags. She pressed a warm rag over my eye. I felt Jamie tugging at my sleeve, heard him crying into the crook of his elbow. Aunt Sarah had her massive dough arms around him, whispering. We both took something from each other that day.

Vern's words tumbled into the backseat with cigarette smoke. I'll always remember the stench of Marlboro Reds.

'You're okay Blakey, you hear? Don't go squealing over a flesh wound. God gave you one peeper too many,' he said. It'd take more than a blinded child to shake a man in Harmswood, Arkansas. Out of the blood and the mucus, out of my brother's tears, Vern's hands and Maw's silence. Out of a gasoline-soaked rag, the smell of pine and a condom we thought was snakeskin. The Bald-Knob fell into the new world and found me unarmed, a child playing in the woods. He flew into the quarry formed by my split eye and perched there waiting to gorge. His talons tapped my skull. Ever since the accident, I've known that part of me has been coddled in the shadow of his wingspan. Jamie's twig pierced an eyeball, skewered the pupil, turned it milky like a snow globe. Turned part of me nocturnal.

THE HOWLERS

He calls it the nothing-door.

It's a womb, a cave, a hole in the ground. He walks for miles through the woods. Then a little further and a littler further each time after that. In some ways it finds him before he finds it. Always slightly shifted, never twice the same. There are ruins in the middle of the forest that no one in Harmswood talks about, best forgotten—like guilt. Jamie started going there after the accident. There are other things too, growing out of the soil. He keeps going back. Back into the pinewood, into the womb. He pushes what grows through the soil into his mouth. Stares through the nothing-door, sleeps in the ruins.

The forest stretches out over acres. Runs behind the corn, cotton, and rye fields. It grinds up against the town, until it touches the roots of the mountain, whose three peaks are called The Teeth. The further in Jamie goes, the more everything vanishes from his memory. The air comes up real close. All is reduced to twigs crunching beneath his feet, twists knotting the bark. The treetops sigh. Jamie is never scared. A thin line splits town from wilderness. When he steps over it, he feels himself grow lighter. Hollowed out, carved from an antler. As if carried by the hands of a moon goddess, dragged through moth wings into her embrace. The wild pulls him out of himself. He doesn't understand the addiction. But it is enough. Enough to make him go back and leave the world behind. Growing smaller, meeker. Eyes in headlights. A tail between the legs. He saw them. They saw him. Since that day, a pact was made. Since that day, he's been their quarry.

The deeper he goes, the less he needs his eyes. He shuts them and the world becomes velvety, he allows himself to glide softly inwards. The more he chews on what grows from the soil, the more he glows with a trapped light. He imagines the black velvet circling him as a panther, who offers him her tail and guides him to the nothing-door, as a long-lost cub. A panther in the leaves, in the creek; that whispers and whistles and calls to him from the tall grass.

It started after the accident—the need to follow that whistle. He never thinks back to it much, partly because he was too young then, too tender. More like a color than a memory. Red and black brushstrokes over the eyes. In the Ozarks folk call panthers *painters*. He'd seen a black shape move away where his brother stood. It walked away into the pines with its back turned. Jamie knew that if he didn't do something it would expand forever and trap all light—all life. He threw the stick to silence it, never to hurt Blake.

There were nights after that when he woke up in the woods. His body slumped over a carpet of roots and foliage. The close smell of animal. Somehow taken before he chose to leave. It happened slowly, as a flower unfolding in moonlight. Nobody saw them. Nobody saw them take him away. Nostrils flared over his small body, many hands. Thick fingers prying and poking into his ribs, tracing the length of his spine from neck to tailbone. Nude. Always skin, skin and parts hanging. Many times, he was lifted out of the nest by strong arms and Blake had his back turned. Outside. Outside on his back. In his pajamas he saw antlers against the sky. Everything changed at night. The old ways were reborn.

It was a child's dream when something snorted into his hair. When something large pulled his cheeks wide. He wouldn't cry. After the accident he swore he would never cry again. Many times, he felt lifted from the top bunk. In the air; over the farm, the fields, the scrapyard, the church steeple. Even with his eyes closed he knew what was mapped out beneath him. Pines. Musk. Dung. Blood-caked fur. He wasn't afraid. It was just another thing that happened out there. They knew to work through the breath of sleep, these dreams did. They knew to pluck cubs from dens with grace and take them in deep. How to whistle like big intelligent cats from the tall grass, from behind tree trunks. Jamie has been looking for them ever since. The masked furies that chose him over everyone else in the shit town. He was theirs. Their cub.

He would wake up slumped face down on the covers. Sweat-drenched. Back inside on the top bunk, smelling of soil and wet earth. The window opened more than it should be. He was only little then. Skin raw and scraped, buzzing in places—throbbing with red. But he was never scared, he always wanted to go back to them. Blake looked up from the bottom bunk with his big bandaged head and couldn't say a word. When Jamie saw the Howlers, it was the richest of silences.

THE BALD-KNOB

Language was conceived by observing the flight patterns of birds.

The cult of the dead thought they were mounts for Saturn and Chronos.

They signaled astral flight.

BLAKE

I had ringing in my ears growing up. Before I uttered my first words. Something larger sat behind them. Crouched, watching. The old folk called themselves Creation-Critters. Their stories were like skinny fences to keep out the wolves. They whispered and laughed in our ears toothlessly, reeking of wet dog. The old people of Harmswood seemed to dwell in the roots of the place, chasing their tails like dumb pups repeating themselves. They were pure Ozark from way before the asphalt was laid down. Before everything was connected, they were inland islanders. They believed they could blow snuff up a woman's nose to make her conceive a child. The creation-critter's offspring worked or got drunk, or drank and didn't work at all.

    I used to try and figure out the stories they told. To make them work in my mind like other stories did. I tried to pull them together by tearing them apart but these words were full of soil and bone. They bit back and had crows cawing inside of them. They had no beginning, middle or end. You were just dropped into them, an egg fallen from some high nest, splattered into a strange new land. Nothing else there but the truth of it. Broken things, feral things born of the last moments before dusk. Reality didn't apply there in the same way it did to other places. Reality was a kind of choice. A feeling in the gut.

When two bodies knock together, they make a strange sound. Muffled. Thudding. So much gets in the way of what wants to meet. What wants to combine and embrace. So much fodder. I made that sound less real through living in stories. I pushed it out of my head with other noises, other voices that sang for me, pummeled my heart, trampled over it with hooves. I lusted for the cacophony, for the bands and the books that kept away the sound of bodies climbing inside one another. The Bald-Knob perched up in the corners of my room, waiting for the night to die so he could dig in. He was always good like that, a patient creature. Two bodies knocking together sounded like furniture after a while.

From the top of the stairs, I heard one of Maw's men yell out after he was done with her. Burning in moonshine brought down from the stills. He got up out of his armchair in a trance, his voice droned, his eyes were fixed on something beyond her, beyond our living room, beyond his swimming skull. He stood legs apart and swayed, like a reed in the wind, until he was completely still, his spine straight as anything. With a whoop he cried:

> *'I am the old original iron-jawed, brass-mounted, copper-bellied, corpse maker from the wilds of Arkansas. I take nineteen alligators and a barrel of whisky for breakfast. Blood's my natural drink and the wails of the dying are music to my ears.'*

He was saluting someone, paying tribute to some general in a life he'd never lived—prowling along beside him. He gargled and collapsed back into the chair like a heap of linen. A thick vein split his forehead, a string of saliva dangled. The glass rolled softly from his hand onto the rug and Maw scoffed, shook her head and took the bottle from between his legs. In the Ozarks all poets drank and died unnoticed.

***

The healing process for my eye was long because it never fully healed. We lived out in the sticks, everything spread out in constellations. The out-of-town doctor was lost with me. Scared of blood and children and bloody children. We went back and forth to Little Rock in the early days, back and forth between scalpels like bees to flowers. It was the quacks and their sharp blades, their endless tunneling, that killed my sight, did away with it for good. I could still see something before that last cut, light dancing through water. I was sliced and sewn up over and over until I went under for the last time at sixteen. When I woke there was no more light dancing.

I had my head bandaged all the way through childhood. I couldn't see a thing for months. My world was a web of touch and scent, of feeling the wrong things in the wrong places. Maw's hoarse twang in the dark. Her lighter and the tobacco squealing were my ball of string in the labyrinth for evading monsters. The front door opened and banged shut. Jamie turned over in his sleep. I listened closely to the world after dark. It's how I heard all the men, all the time. Maw shifting through phases like the moon, dark eating into the light. She scared me because parts of her were inside me. Because those parts made us bigger than Harmswood. She was more than her childhood ever allowed her to be. My mother choked me. Spoke as if she was planning to get the gutters cleared. Liquor coated her voice, lubricated her tongue. She described the world back and made it sound frightening. She held my hand to skewer the food on my plate as she talked about the crops dying. I heard tapping on the windowpane and knew they were fingertips.

Once or twice the window would open. Once or twice, I heard

Jamie move off into the open air. Springs sang in his mattress. They couldn't keep him indoors. The forest always talked back to us Ackermans. My brother stayed at aunt Sarah's through those first months. It was like every time he looked at my face, he didn't see me anymore. He saw whatever it was that stared back through the trees. Whatever it was that made the world go black on that day. I knew the facts but not the truth of it. Never the truth. Maw was glad to see him sent off. I remember the sound of the car that took him. I remember him screaming behind the glass.

'One minute he's climbing the walls. Next, he's collapsed on the floor and won't move for hours. Like someone turned the lights out in his head. Just lies there under a blanket. Sarah tried to wash the thing once and he bit her hand to the bone, the little bastard,' Maw said. 'He's a devil. He ain't good like you are,' she said. I didn't see my brother for months.

When the bandages came off there were faces everywhere. Faces in harvesters, eyes in tree-bark. The headlights and bumper on every pickup were a hyena. Our dead dogs were in the clouds chasing each other. Leftovers on a plate became wailing portraits and melting masks. I grew superstitions for protection. I pictured black cats exploding into flames while they licked pearly-white claws, ignoring me. I now know that these are conditions with big names: *Pareidolia, Apophenia*. Music out of noise, connecting dots that aren't there. There were no explanations back then. Just omens. In Harmswood, the Devil was in everything you didn't understand. I kept picturing cats explode to protect myself from more accidents.

My left eye had turned blue. The Bald-Knob hatched from that cold blue egg. It had no pupil. Little white fragments dotted around like splintered porcelain. The greatest advice given to me in those early days was by a doctor called Gunner, a man in his fifties with a damp voice and yellow fingers from rolling tobacco. Doctor Gunner had the air of a survivor. Like he'd fallen through a slit in time, transported from a battlefield somewhere, his head full of cannon fire, fumes and sabers clashing. He held my face in his hands under a surgical lamp. Twisted it this way and that as our shadows merged on the floor and grew heads, wings and tails. There was something about these visits that calmed me. The tingling feeling all through my body, like a wave of caterpillars walking along the branch of my limbs. Gunner told me to read everything I could get my hands on and strengthen the sight in my good eye. 'Consume it all kid. Keep pumping blood between the ears. Be greedy with it,' he said after each visit.

I spent most days at the public library. A building no one figured out the use of. Damp stains on the walls, buckets on the floor to catch water from broken pipes in the ceiling. Desks and chairs were piled on top of each other in the far corner. Shoals of silverfish shot out from under books like meteor showers looking for the closest pools of shadow. Sue Batty was the sole employee. She did everything from archiving to emptying those buckets of brown ceiling water. At first, she would give me books that were too old and tattered for distribution. But, in the end, she just offered them up anyway.

'Who else'll take them? At least you've got the hunger,' she said squeezing my shoulder. I took heaps of dog-eared novels that all fell apart and spent nights gluing spines back to pages. Sue wore her husband's cardigan as if it were the pelt of an animal she'd slain. She was a haunted person. Never mentioned the loggerhead. Her husband had been a janitor at our school. After their kid died, he was on the whiskey most days and, when he was dry, he bribed us boys with cigarettes for a few sips of our jungle juice. A blend of soda with whatever liquor could be stolen from home, disguised by a carton with some young woman that had seashells for a bra. Carl had snakes driving him. One summer he appeared from nowhere and sat down with me and my brother by the lake. He gave us beers and pulled a bent joint from behind his ear. Yellow-eyed, burst blood vessels on the tip of his nose. The light played with our minds and the water felt good. We tilted cans back and the grass smelled sour. Carl always had a hoarse voice like he'd been hollering all night for someone to hear.

'That there's a mark of God,' he said, while we dunked our feet in the shallows. I shrugged. Jamie punched my shoulder, pulled my arm for us to go but I couldn't move. 'I bet you can see everything we can't,' he said and pinched me on the earlobe. I never saw him again. He hanged himself in the boys' locker room. I read up on all the gods. On Odin. It took a while getting under my skin. I had to push through a membrane, against everything pulling me out into the fields. Certain fragments of text started sticking to my mind, like deer ticks. Moving, still alive, fighting for air in my consciousness. They buried themselves deep enough to a point where I could always feel the vibrations of their kicking legs. Through that language I could spin myself into a flock of starlings, transport into the mind of a stag and inhabit all types of weather.

At school I was shamed for being an Ackerman. Both of us were. I had my face pushed in a toilet bowl and my arms bent back so far I thought they might pop. The more I read, the more I found I could be there and elsewhere, I could divide myself up into more than one person. A passage from E L Doctorow's *Ragtime* was tattooed onto my sense of self. What it could mean through the music of words. It referred to stories from Ovid, whose name sounded unknowable, old and attractive to me all at once. Black licorice, endlessly dissolving in my mouth. It went:

> *People who became animals or trees, or statues. They were stories of transformation. Women turned into sunflowers, spiders, bats, birds; men turned into snakes, pigs, statues and even thin air. The forms of life were volatile and everything in the world could easily be something else.*

I read the paragraph over and over again to the point where I could taste it. The language devoured me and I found a connection in the hinterland, the aftermath of my accident. I felt advanced beyond my years, outside of time. Beyond the speck of dust that was our town. I studied flocks of starlings when they flew in huge swarms over the cotton fields in early winter, casting their fishing nets in the sky. I wondered whether they were many beating hearts or my own pulse. Now I knew they could be both, they could be one beautiful word: Murmuration.

For the rest of my childhood any life beyond words, myths and music felt thin. At night creatures that prowled around outside in the forest moved inside me also. Calling out to each other over the acres as I lay on my bottom bunk with a blinking flashlight. I clutched at novels with red fingers, leaving sweat marks on each page. My little brother talked in his sleep. The mattress creaked when he turned over. Maw played Lead Belly records downstairs, deep into the night. In those early days I would follow the black marks like ant trails around each page like I was mapping out the stars. Beneath Jamie with his fire and his guilt and the wolves coming for him every night—I was there reading. The vessels in my right eye filled with blood and each hour rolled over into the next until white noise turned into birdsong.

TALL BOYS

Since Jamie was little, he's drawn the same three stick-men in the corners of every journal. Three men with broad shaggy bodies, hair hanging down from the arms. They wear masks with horns, antlers, and hollow cut-out eyes. He draws them with knives, hatchets, and rope in their hands that they hold up to the sky. Swing over theirs heads in lassos. If he still had the journals and Maw hadn't hidden them away in one of her fits—there'd be an entire hoard sprawled in the margins. When he had a red pen handy, he would scribble swirls and zig-zag lines around them like they'd caught fire. The smell of singed flesh rose off the page.

Everything he knew stuck to the skin. Especially the smell of love. There was a moment, before Blake left Harmswood, when life was a little lighter. It was by accident that Jamie fell for an older boy. At school they sat side by side. Neil 'Bull' Hughes was kept back a year or so. He leant back in his chair, singeing the wood under the belly of his desk with a lighter so that the whole classroom stank of his bitter boredom. Jamie was made to sit next to him in detention. Back then Bull was only a minor criminal, got himself a reputation for dealing ditch-weed and stealing propane canisters from neighbors in the trailer park. He was strong, muscular even at that age. Taller than the rest. A bully for boys that were *other*.

The adults in charge sat Jamie next to Bull because they were cruel people. They knew what happened in the corridors and the restrooms. That he was held down and cigarettes were put out on his arms. That he was tripped up, his crooked legs flailing in the air like an upturned beetle. Jammed in a locker until his arms went blue. Bull pointed to his legs. Sniggering, called him a hobgoblin. Blake was in the library. Blake was unaware. Blake had this happen to him only twice before Maw took him out of school. Scared for her baby boy. Sometimes forked tongues pierced deeper than knives did. Neither of them could have foreseen how for a time the world got turned on its head. How sometimes the white void outshines darkness.

Junior high was when it started. One afternoon, Jamie was sent to detention for fish-hooking a kid in the cheek. He'd found a way of getting behind them, locking his legs around the thighs, and falling backwards. They couldn't move, it was like watching a leopard take out a gazelle. At the back of class, he was hunched over biting his hand between index and thumb. Jamie sat down and Bull sucked his teeth loudly. They said nothing. As moments passed, in the funny bone of minutes, Jamie felt Bull's thigh nudged against his. It was gentle. For once it wasn't the beginning of violence. The older boy placed himself there like a thermos, his body heat slipped through the pores and Jamie tasted him through the skin like a snake. Hot as the chili powder Aunt Sarah laid outside her chicken coop to keep away foxes and evil spirits.

The tall boy pushed in further. He rubbed up and down until Jamie did the same and together they made heat, they made light, they made flame. They sat like that until the end of class. Upper body rigid, while their legs did the footwork. Never looking at each other, never daring. With each detention they grew hungrier. Elbows and arms were the next threshold. No one paid them attention. No one figured out that boys could yearn for a womb-warmth. That they could be each other's otherness. Towards the end of that year, they discovered that dragging fingernails over each other's skin made it electric and the meaning of life became waiting for detention. The meaning of life was bred inside those tingling points.

It caused a split in Jamie. But he understood that there was night and there was day and the two had to co-exist and be hidden from each other. Outside he was still Chicken Legs, he was still an Ackerman. Bull still jeered and shoulder-barged him but with a feather-lightness he grew to accept. He went out of his way to make Bull feel large. Like a skull-crusher and a body-mangler. In the eyes. It was always in the eyes. But not under the desk. Not behind the bike sheds. Not in the restrooms with the cigarette butts and hurried unbuckling and the kisses that tasted of grape jelly. Not in the anguish of coming too quickly or in the relief when it didn't matter. After a year went by, they would meet in the ruins of the old school, out in the pinewood.

Blake was in the fields, driving around with Vern when Bull picked Jamie off the street like a rag-doll. The old school was haunted. When he stepped inside, a wood-pigeon burst through the shadows. Jamie started trashing the place to impress. Bull liked his anger, the way it flowered over everything. He stood back smoking as a sink smashed against the wall. The rows of beds were left untouched. It felt wrong to disturb the children's rooms. The whole floor was covered in porn magazines, they lit them up with lighter fluid and the night was pushed back by the burning of naked women. Jamie'd found his sanctum. There they could be everything they needed to be. The split was real. The transformation of it was something Jamie felt thrumming deep inside. A softening in the eyes was what made Bull real to him, the shift as his shoulders dropped and his jaw loosened. From enemy to lover in the world's blind spot. This was their nest. The only place they were permitted wings.

'You're the woman though,' Bull demanded in a shaky way before anything happened. There had to be that space between them still, to know he still had power. Jamie thought of cracked bare feet over bitumen, ripped clothes and the sound of tires squealing in the night. The wheels made him wonder how many women the men had to make up to keep them company, to be whole. He wondered what would happen if everyone simply surrendered to the unstoppable pulse. In Harmswood you had to crawl inside something else to be yourself, you had to wear a mask with antlers and long mouths. Deer hung upside down, gutted out in Jamie's memory when he answered.

'Sure, I'm the woman,' he'd say. This wasn't like he'd heard it at home; rough, glum, unwilling. Bull was rubbery. Eel-like. He made Jamie's body feel fluid, circular, erupting again and again. Articulated and no longer grotesque. It made sense. Jamie's hands knew what to do, his tongue knew what to do, the unnameable part of him knew what to do. Like it had happened in other lifetimes. With Bull all the things fit and bolted tightly. For a year, Jamie stopped drawing the three men on fire in the corner of every page. For a time, all the noise of home was turned down to such a low frequency, he could barely hear it squeak. Even Blake. Even Blake was squeezed from his mind like a zit.

In senior year the split cracked wider. Bull fell in deep with the Peckerwood gangs. He vanished. Jamie roamed around the trailer park searching, madly hoping. He waited for long hours after school at the usual time, at the usual place by steps covered in ivy, grass growing through the stone. Jamie even prayed. For the first time in his life, he prayed that some things were too big to go unseen. He waited out there in the smoky chill of fall until he shook all over. Until his teeth chattered and the whiskey froze solid in the bottle after the sun fell. He waited until his heart became a fledgling with its mouth wide open, until his eyes stung and tingled with pain right up to the roots. The next time Jamie saw Bull was inside Griffin's trailer. He came to buy rocks without shooting him a glance. Jamie followed him outside, to ask why, to ask how, to ask if, and was knocked down with a knee to the groin. Called a faggot, loudly, so it echoed. So loudly it made the dogs whine. So loudly it made hate simple.

The look in Bull's eyes was shame, a white anger as Jamie held himself coughing into the mud. The tall boy rocked on the balls of his feet hollering abuse, Jamie knew he'd lost. Bull was being groomed. Groomed for what some men called manhood. Plucked from mange-ridden fur like a fat flea. They never had a chance. Out there, wings were clipped early, before anyone knew they had them. He walked away and let the youth scream behind him. Never told Blake, it didn't seem right. Shortly after that, Bull got arrested for arson and spent four years in the state penitentiary.

Jamie started dealing. Started snorting H, started lacing his cigarettes, and bubbling powder in a spoon until it caramelized. Anything he had at hand to tear down the emotion and obliterate it, anything to forget about how life was once tingling points of flame at the back of a classroom. Blake left his Walkman behind on the day he fled Harmswood. Sitting there in the middle of a mattress, all the records spread around like a headdress. Jamie hid the earphones under his floppy hair and listened to the tapes in a loop until the day was done. Slowly the three men came back. They started spilling from the page like fire ants. They bled over onto the desk, swarming over the empty surface, scorching it over and over, swallowing up the furniture. Jamie stopped wanting to live after Blake left. His three flaming men stormed off the page and all the world was just firewood waiting to happen.

THE BALD-KNOB

In Rome criminals were condemned to be eaten alive by wild animals.

Inside each man's skull is a bird's nest.

Damnatio et Bestias—until the nest bursts.

BLAKE

Buzzards were everywhere when I was little. They circled in kettles and fed in wakes. The sky was pregnant with their silhouettes. Earth bristled as they sunned their wings, stretched out to burn away bacteria. We knew they had acid in their guts strong enough to melt bone. It was our way of disposing of that which would otherwise fester. Settlers used to feed the vultures their dead—it was a way of keeping the balance. A way of getting the soul out before it got trapped. A man did what he could to keep his name clean. I knew this—it was drilled into me. My uncle told me to keep it close to my heart like the picture of a saint. Our name meant we always kept the balance.

It was crop-burning season when I understood what the birds were for, that they were death-eaters. Growing up, they were familiar, they blended in. Pinned to the sky. A crooked heap in the corner of your eye. Pitch-black with a flesh-red head. Scalped, as if the feathers had been burnt away there. They had witch's toes and hatched their chicks in the tar pit of caves. I wonder about this, with the distance I've put between myself and the past. Whether the trench I've dug is deep enough. I wonder about what we did out there with my uncle, all those times with no eyes watching. How it is skin, mist, and the smell of wet earth. My memories have dissolved. Dug up moments that are still happening. Fossils, kicking at the web like flies. Everything I did with Vern in the woods was waste disposal. Watching things break down. I remember the beginning of the end as the color turquoise.

Diclofenac Sodium was a powder that for a brief moment felt like hope for our small town. Sweet and precious as candy. The state recruited able-bodied men to work the plant. They arrived from all over Arkansas; a shimmering-milk gleam over the eyes, a hunger. This turquoise powder was a ladder out of poverty. Out of scraping crops from the earth that made the stomach turn and the mind swirl. The new cattle drug was on the tip of every farmer's tongue. It numbed the animals out. Enough to ignore wounds and deformities. They didn't need sleep anymore. Turquoise is the color of cunning, venom, and patterns on the backs of amphibians. It screamed but no one heard it.

Everyone blamed the birds when the powder crept into the meat and turned it black. When the cattle started flopping over and dying, they were inedible to the vultures. Their acid couldn't break it down. It started killing them too. They dropped their heads like wilted flowers and thudded from telephone wires onto the asphalt. They lay down next to roadkill and became one with it. With the vultures gone, pestilence spread. Vern's herd slimmed down to a skeletal few. Folk didn't realize that the powder was burning through their livestock like wildfire. It got into the drinking water and by the end claimed the entire bovine population of Harmswood. The name Ackerman lost all meaning. The balance was lost. The fields went silent. Everyone blamed the birds.

On the night before the end of the world, Vern sat at our kitchen table with a glass of whiskey, chain-smoking Marlboro Reds. All pink in the eyes. My uncle stared through the space between himself and everything else as if it were hell's chasm. His lips quivered. The screen-door banged in the late blue breeze, drops from the faucet fell into a saucepan as God kept time there in our kitchen. I stood in front of him, but his eyes didn't budge, he couldn't see me. My brother growled and pressed thumbs against the side of his head fanning the fingers out like antlers. Still Vern was not there with us. He was with ghosts, in the dirt, with his eyes and mouth sewn shut.

Maw was outside singing to the trees. Her hands moved in ten-tacles and crescent moons. I heard a tapping on the windowpane that night and crushed my face deep in the pillow. Maw never interfered when it came to Vern. Never spoke up. As twins they didn't need to say much, it had all been said before in a cave far away. As dawn broke, Vern took me with him to put down the last few heifers and the old bull. I'd never seen him so faded. It was early fall and everything was cloaked in a fog of crops seething which clogged up our sinuses. His sandpaper hand shook me awake. Lips next to my ear. I was told to wash and meet him by the truck. The stench of wet manure hung at the back of my throat. I left Jamie curled up on the top bunk, nestled. Sleep cracked my eyes and Vern had his back to me. I squinted at his shoulders rising and falling under the rhinoceros skin of denim. He breathed like something snared. We drove, as we always drove and my heart was a hummingbird. The sun jabbed its fingers through the pines. The world was so loud with everybody else sleeping.

We reached our family plot. There was a small cluster of an-imals over the way, in the middle of the field, huddled together like defenseless children. My uncle turned to me.

'This here is what God's done to us,' he said a little shaky. 'He don't ask—he just takes. My Daddy scraped every last cent he had to buy the first bull. He went without to buy that damn bull,' he yanked on the handbrake like a tearing off a rib, sat back and closed his eyes for a few moments. Wind shook the truck. He snorted and started pushing bullets into a pistol with his thumb. One and then the next. Dog tags hung from the mirror and caught the morning light as gunshots cracked the sky. As he murdered his children, I traced faces in the clouds. Prayed hard for the grace of a murmuration that never came. The engine ground me up into pebbles as I waited. Through the rearview I saw pale bulks still heaving from turquoise plague. Bones rose up into the skin like tents. Foghorns from foaming mouths, almost human. Vern loped between them, his gun dangled. He scratched the back of his neck until it was raw. Eyes drawn deep in his skull from disbelief.

I watched him walk up to each cow, breathe, and pull the trigger. Over and over. Until it became fast, manic—he missed and mud fountained. I watched as ice hardened in his veins. The last thirteen he killed on that day and kept coming back to reload. Fumes spiraled, empty shells rolled onto the floor by my feet. Every moment was lead-filled. Breath lodged into my windpipe like fish bones. The moon was still out as nature's clean-up crew descended. Black-feathered, scarlet-headed making slits wide enough to hear the organs whisper.

Vern looked up to the sky when it was done. All teeth and saliva. The old bull was last to go. Shot behind the ear. I saw him say something and tried to read his lips. The light was fleshy pink now, the stomach lining of fall. His eyes went through me like harpoons. In that moment I saw him reliving many little deaths. Somewhere blood petalled from chests, limbs twisted and dried out like tobacco leaves. A field of souls squealed for their mothers, clutched at their insides as they spilled. Shot through the throat, the gut, the groin. Metal clicking under boot, triggers, and fire. Creatures he'd birthed, gelded, killed. Children. The land felt bare.

Slumped in the truck, he squeezed the wheel. The thin hair on his head danced like reeds underwater. I reached into his pocket and shook a cigarette out, pushed it into his mouth, and lit it with a match in small circles. This I could always do, I could light the fuse for anyone about to implode. The hiss of it broke the ice. As the smoke spiraled, he let his head drop.

'The questions they asked us after Nam were wrong. Their words were like fridges tossed down a hill. There are no answers. When you knock on that door and it opens, there's only darkness and loud noises. There's wild animals in there. You peer in but there's no way you're walking into that room, you bow your head, back away and pull the door shut,' he said and a deep welt formed under his cheekbone, his eyes went coffee-bean black. The door he'd been holding shut was nudged open on that day. All those animals were testing the air with flicking tongues and wet noses. It was the only time my uncle mentioned Vietnam. In a truck full of red smoke with vultures landing. The moment is still happening.

Whenever I close my good eye, a snake eats its tail.

MEN LIKE ME

The things no one wants to see—Jamie's always seen. It's been hard. Sight is what gives a person their dreams. Jamie loves Blake. He loves him for his forgiveness and yet loathes every second of being forgiven. Unable to focus. Burning, burning alive every day with the shame of it. He can never un-see, un-feel, un-know. Flames eat his heart up like a paper boat. The fights got bad after Blake left.

He couldn't stay with Maw anymore. Her men stumbled into the walls and furniture as she cooed around them with ice ringing in her glass. They tripped over the rug, grabbed at their belts fumbling and cursing. She was a kind of balm to them. Peeled off each layer like dead skin until they were naked, skinned alive, hollering in ecstasy. Harmswood is a veteran's town, men numb themselves but the war rages on. Maw fed on her men, without them she flickered and faded out. When they were done with her, she stopped existing. They always left stuff lying around—cash, hash, flasks of liquor. The moonshiners loved Ma.

When God took a long piss, Harmswood sprouted from the hard earth. Jamie hung small wooden crosses in his bedroom and turned them upside down. He liked that God was watching, biting his nails. He collected leftovers from the Burt-Mill cemetery. Stole things left for loved ones. Stored them in the house, in holes under the bridge that he later dug up with his bare hands. He knew that God was watching. Sin made him feel strong. It put the spring in his chest. Gravestones cracked with age. People's names faded, weeds grew up through the bones.

Playing dead was Jamie's weapon. Maw changed when she saw the crosses. It was the crosses that tipped her. Like roaches, vermin, like all unwelcome guests. On the last day he spent at home, she lost her mind. She pulled the drawers out limb from limb, gutted all the closets. She collected the crosses and dried up flowers and stuffed them all into a shoebox. Jamie stiffened while she tore through each room muttering to invisible strangers. He stood in the middle of the kitchen, waiting, feeling chaos whisper through the floorboards above him. There were days when his mother had nine monstrous heads. They sprouted when each man left. She came down, grabbed him, and he went limp, it was always this way after the accident. Nothing more than a black box at the back of his skull sucking everything into it. Nothing more than a nothing door. He had been transported through his brother's wound. Through that split in the pupil. That snake in the eye. Blake was out with Vern again.

'Why are you so wrong? Why are you so damn cruel to me?' she said, squeezing his ears. 'I've never needed you, none of you. All animals is what you are, all filth and mange and swallowing.' He wouldn't answer. There was nothing to say that she would understand, she was never interested in understanding.

'Get down there.' This is what she did. What she always did. Pulled his hair back. Told him to open up. Poured lye soap down his throat. He learnt to stare at patches of damp on the ceiling. Up at the places where it started to peel away and curl into centipedes— some shapes looked like countries far away. When the light was right, he'd spot the arrowheads of birds in migration as they flashed through the window, going somewhere, anywhere else. That was the day Maw stopped for good. She stopped being God when Jamie opened his mouth up wider to help her. He pushed his tongue out and stared at her, into all the layers of her as she poured the soap down into him. Her pupils shrunk as if light had hit them. Her hands loosened. She dropped him to the floor gasping and puking and never touched him again. But the sun can't reach certain areas of the deep.

He ran off to Griffin's trailer after that. Slept on his floor for a month. The trailer park was good for laying low. As long as you kept your head down. Griffin was simple—all blotches and grease. Looked older than he was, sunken and hollow-cheeked, little brown scars from infected piercings. They talked about girls because they had to. Jamie knew that Griffin had never been with a woman from the way his voice went higher, from how he kept uncrossing his legs. Living with Maw taught Jamie some things of the flesh, how to sniff out the boys from the men.

Griffin's thing was tattoos. But he was no good. Homemade guns from guitar wire and cheap pen ink. He had a bunch of crowns and misspelled words scrawled over his thighs for practice. Trailer trash loved their royalty. He got the idea after his Daddy came out of the penitentiary. He listened to every word his Daddy spoke. He did the ink for members of the skinhead gangs. Let them hang out smoking rocks while he drilled into their bodies. Blood swirling in with the dark ink. Griffin's Dad trusted Jamie to push H for a while. From time to time, he had to go away and disappear. Jamie chain-smoked in the corner handing out sachets of brown powder for cash. He watched their eyes mist over. Glassy, tin-foiled under a flickering fluorescent bulb.

Sometimes he couldn't stand Griffin. Couldn't stand the sour smell in the trailer, unwashed clothes in piles. Wires poking through the wall got to him. He started getting that urge, that snarl in the chest. 'Can you ink a man to death?' a small voice whispered. 'Cross him out for good.' He shook his head to clear it. Took off before something leapt out of him and into Griffin, going for the voice-box, the heart, the eyeballs. Before he took the little tattoo gun and started blackening him out of sight, scribbling him away. Griffin was a dumb kid but a good person. Jamie hid his violence in a sigh.

Mary-Anne Bowery took him in. Thought of him as her boyfriend. They'd known each other since the dog bit her. The third of the six did it. He was a beast, small but snaggletoothed. Vern brought him home one evening half-mangled by coyotes or something bigger. Jamie liked the dog even though it could never be pet. Still like a statue. It'd face the woods and stay there all day watching, ears pricked to attention. They kept him tied up all day and at night let him loose barking himself into a frenzy. Barking into nothing. Into everything.

When she was little, Mary-Anne walked all the way to the farm from town. She wanted to see where he lived. In a little floral dress, the sun through her hair. Jamie was still living at Sarah's then. He'd have protected her otherwise, he'd have put himself between her and the large gaping mouth. She was bit bad in the face, all over the legs. Vern put him down and everything seemed louder without him barking. Dumped out by the pines.

Mary-Anne was pretty. Even with the scars. Surgeries couldn't erase them. Carved into her cheekbone. Curved up around the eye socket. Jamie enjoyed listening to her, the feeling of being wanted. Her house was the fanciest in town, old colonial. One of the only ones left standing after the mines collapsed. Wind chimes on the porch. A flag erect. Sprinklers in the yard that stopped working two summers back. Her father liked everything painted white. One of the only men in Harmswood that didn't visit Ma. Mary-Anne liked Jamie because his name was dirty. If her Daddy knew what she got up to, he'd have Jamie thrown in the hole. Jamie threw stones at her window and crept in like a fox to a crib. She pulled him in close by the belt. Pulled him to her hips and he tensed, looking to the corners for peeling wallpaper and centipedes. Looking to the sky for arrowheads. It always came easy showing her the colors in herself, the hidden shapes. It made her breath scatter and her eyes roll back in her skull like boiled eggs. He glided out of his body and stood in the corner waiting for it to end. He could give nothing. He climbed out before sunrise and pulled a water sprinkler out of the earth like a root vegetable.

The library is where he ended up. He lay on his back under a desk next to the fire exit. Sue Batty looked out for him, tried to. Told him he wasn't a tramp, that people talked when they didn't want to listen. A lump formed in his throat whenever she spoke. Sue Batty never threw him out, only repeated herself until even the sound of her words became dust rising. Jamie stacked books for a pillow as she flicked each light switch off one by one, locked him in for the night. Something in her movements was so achingly human.

Folk tales came alive, creaked like small wooden animals in the dark. Walked at his side, knuckle over fist, antlers and heavy breathing. You always smelt them first. Musk, the wilderness coated thickly. Jamie tried going home once, after the first month of sleeping rough. A long walk without a ride. Asphalt for forty-five minutes on foot until he turned right down the dirt road, all after sunset. He left it late as possible. On that walk his footsteps were slow. When there were no cars on the road, no stars in the sky, when all he heard were insects, he closed his eyes and pretended to be on a high-wire thousands of miles up in the air. Nothing else, only him perched on the wire, stretched over an abyss with his eyes closed. Warm as a ball of clay in practiced hands. Strange how H changed the pattern of pain. Like staring into headlights until all that darkness was pushed far out to the rim.

He opened his eyes to find he'd strayed into the center of the asphalt. If a car'd been coming the other way he'd be done, flattened. A carcass dried out by the sun. Those weren't headlights he saw, they were a single fire-bug. The only light in the world; no stars, no moon. A speck that bobbed and left behind a crooked tail. When Jamie moved closer, he saw that it wasn't an insect but an ember followed by footsteps. Panting, a familiar wheeze in the lungs. A honk and spit fell to the earth close by. Jamie pulled his zippo out and moved the flame into the dark until it trapped Vern's face. The light bucked in front of his uncle like a newborn foal.

Vern stopped, swaying. His face, a haggard mask tight over the bones. Beaten by the weather. With heavy lids he looked straight into the flame. Jamie took a step closer moving the zippo up and down the length of him. His uncle was in woman's clothes. Tight woman's clothes. A white tank top ripped in places, his hands silvery and blackened from coal or ash, clumps of green-brown dirt pasted on a short denim skirt. When Jamie looked down, he saw bare feet cracked and bloodied. His uncle's eyes were plastered with mascara. Thick lipstick smudged across his mouth, caught in needles of sharp stubble. Jamie swallowed hard. They stood like sculptures, chests swelling and collapsing. The wolves that lived in Jamie's stomach put back their ears. The wounds on his uncle's feet, the dried blood, cracked through glimpses of flame. Vern struck a match and moved it in circles over a cigarette. Shaking it away, he coughed before speaking. Vern is what happened after sunset in the Ozarks. What came alive. A wolf in a dress.

'Ma's been shit worried. Am I gonna tell her you've been roaming around doing favors for drug-rats? That might just be the death of her,' he said. His voice hard on the ear. A sour tang of whiskey. Jamie put away the lighter.

'They say you've a woman keeping you busy,' said Jamie nodding. 'This her?'

Vern grabbed him. A thumb pushed into the throat.

'You've always been a slut,' he said. 'A turd. It's men like me who keep things right. With the kind of day I've had, shit.' He took deeper drag, nails chipped with turquoise polish. 'You might as well have burnt my own mother alive with the day I've had, you understand, bastard?' he said. 'You tell on me and I'll grind your bones up with the offal,' he said and let go. Jamie couldn't find his heart. The stench of animal gore, whiskey, slaughterhouse took him back to watching men open up bucks when he was little. They'd hang them upside down. Place buckets beneath their heads for the blood. He would stare at their faces, their milky eyes, as hands churned inside them. Hands that could turn all the lights out.

'I say we didn't see each other at all,' said Vern. All Jamie could do was play dead.

'I never saw nothing,' he said hoarsely. Vern took Jamie's head and shoved it into the space between his neck and shoulder.

'It's *men* like *me*,' he said into the side of Jamie's skull, let go, and pushed past him into the night. A moonbeam broke through the clouds and Jamie saw a hillbilly in his fifties wearing the clothes of a young girl. Misshapen, contorted, strangely fierce. The woman that kept him company. Vern always worked with the dirt inside a body. Kept it all locked up behind the glass pane of his eyes. It was wrong to look at him. The adrenaline made Jamie giggle into his hands as he kept walking. Skin-crawled with flight.

When he reached the house, his shoulders were rigid. They'd

nail his uncle's balls to a paw-paw tree if they found out. Maw was on the porch. The living room light shone through her hair. Crickets chirped and tessellated into his fiber; every molecule became a cricket chirping. She fondled a small glass of liquor between her fingers, squinted. Jamie hadn't been back home since the soap and the crosses. All he wanted to do was be with Blake. To listen to him talk about something bigger than this. Something new he'd read. Myths of men transforming into beasts, Vikings, goddesses with snakes for hair. Jamie loved it all, but only through Blake. His brother was good at making words glow in the dark. He walked up to the porch, steps creaking. He still felt Vern's thumbprint on his throat. Ma's teeth ground all of his singing crickets into dust.

'Ma…'

'There's chicken from yesterday,' she said, nodding and brushing ash off her dress. 'Should be hot water, too. I can smell you from here.' She killed her cigarette on the bannister.

'Maw there's—', but before he could say she pushed past him into the house. A door slammed, the wood shuddered. She never wanted to hear it. Jamie pushed through, hoping it was just them. No cars drawing up out of nowhere in the early hours. Blake read next to an open window. Almost a ghost. He turned his head and there it was again. The murky wasteland of his eye. It broke him a little bit more. The pale blue of it, smashed plates. It was love that did it, only love. Jamie moved closer and sunk into the bottom bunk while Blake closed his book smiling.

'Play me a song, man,' he said. Jamie muttered under his breath. He forgot how to respond. 'I've heard you bang out a masterpiece in five minutes. You don't even know how good are,' Blake said, lifting up the old family five-string.

The sixth tuning knob broke off years back. No one had the wherewithal to fix it. That's what you did, you took the hit and adapted to the pain, grew over the wound like a fungus. Jamie started messing around on it back in the early days at Sarah's when his brother was in hospital. Strumming on those strings kept his pulse dancing, harmonics kept breath in his lungs and a kind of column formed, a chord that kept the disparate parts stitched together. It hurt Jamie. Blake's unconditional love. He pushed the guitar away. They spent the hours leaning out of their bedroom window, shooting glances at the pines.

'Maw knows she did wrong. We had words. She knows it was evil this time,' Blake said to Jamie quietly. But all he could think about was Vern, how he couldn't tell, sparks in his skull like firecrackers. Maybe he was just crazy. As a child, he'd tried to take his own eye out with a bush-knife, so that then things would be even. Vern wrestled it out of his hand and slapped his head. He shrugged at his brother.

'Maw and me, man, we'll never be good,' he said. Blake frowned. He moved closer. Brushed a coil of dirty blonde hair away and landed a kiss on his temple. A soft burning rub. He leaned his head on Jamie and his voice vibrated their skeletons.

'Be safe, J. Or this place will eat you. Don't ever be dead meat walking,' he said.

Jamie knew more about the woods than Blake. Felt them inside of him. He saw everything his brother didn't see. When he found the ruins, it was impossible to think about being anywhere else. He didn't stay the night. It was a mistake. Maw fell asleep in the armchair, lips folded in like petals. After half the pack was smoked, after they talked shit and cackled like hyenas, he crept back out into the open. Back to the pinewood. He reached out for the panther's tail. The accident came to define him forever in Harmswood, whose sign read: The Town under The Teeth.

THE BALD-KNOB

Buzzards can scent bodies from beyond the ocean. They can fly high and see much that is concealed by the darkness of mountains. They have no carnal knowledge of the other sex and conceive without semen. Buzzards are able to predict the death of a man by the way he sighs.

BLAKE

Vern bred goats when the cows went. He birthed kids, milked udders, and sliced throats open. The bucks were dehorned and castrated. He didn't like goats, the way they could climb up things was unnatural, the way they were still and stared. Twisted horns and pupils that were all wrong like beans. Jamie and I watched sometimes with hands over our mouths so he wouldn't hear us. Vern was different after I saw him shoot the cattle. He drove out into the black most nights. Growing up, folks said a lot of things about my uncle and Ma. A lot of things about how we were a cursed litter. At times, it felt as if the sinkhole in the middle of the woods was trying to pull everything down into it. Until there was nothing left but birds dropping dead from pylons and old timers clicking their dentures. I read books so many times the voices in those pages were loud as plucked strings.

Our farm was built on a curve off of the asphalt. Dirt trails slunk away into fields. Veiny leftovers from when all the roads were dirt. Dogs guarded us. They were dumb enough to chase anything down. We scraped many from under the wheels and bumpers of pickups, sometimes dragged for miles. After the end of the world, I was at home on the floor with a bandaged head, snapping an arm back into the socket of a green army man. I was at home when I heard the last dog squeal. A car stopped on the road and a man's voice hollered. Another squeal as he accelerated. For a couple of moments, there was silence and an urge swelled within me. I needed to see. I walked out of the house. Down the porch steps. Curled my hands into fists. My head a glass cabinet, thoughts soaked in formaldehyde. Fear nipped at my heels. Fear knocked its head against the glass—again and again—as I pushed one foot out in front of the other.

Six made a weird shape on the asphalt. She had a hind leg turned all the way back. Two buzzards had landed. Pulled at her body. Rocked her like a fishing boat. A small group of crows cawed from the power lines, cheering them on. Crows were larger in Arkansas. They broke into vehicles, smashed through the glass with their beaks. They made themselves known in the world. The turkey vultures spread their wings, opening up their heads into red corridors. Tears burned my cheeks. The largest bird had its foot right over her face pressing her down into the dirt. I stared at my dog's round eyes. I walked up to them, my heart a small balloon. I fought to stay awake, alive, to not be a dead thing. I wanted them to see life and fear it. They hissed, shaking their wings like banners. My whole body hummed. I heard the bark creak in the pines and closed my good eye.

I collapsed. Wherever it was I went. A womb in the mind. A thousand feathery folds.

Nothing. Beat. Nothing. Beat. Wings fanned the dust.

Pressure, tingling, temperature. My eye opened and let the light flood in. Vern stood over me with that same pistol. The life-taker. He must have been watching. All the birds flew up. Erupted like firecrackers. I crawled next to my dog and put my hand on her snout. Hugged her neck. My uncle looked down at me, jerking the pistol around. Lines in his face. His overalls covered in dark mud, sole to belly. A cigarette burned close to the filter in his other hand, teasing out the hair on his knuckles. He looked like a statue in the middle of a square, covered in bird shit. He'd always found me lying on my back, looking up into the shape of him against the sky. My uncle really hated turkey vultures. He was a cattle farmer's son.

'They smell them from miles away,' he said. 'Come knocking like the damn reaper.' Deep wrinkles carved into his forehead like ruts in a field. I stroked Six's head.

'She's mine,' I whispered.

'Yours?' he said under his breath. 'Sometimes I think you're soft as soft goes. I'll show you why nothing is ever *yours*,' he said. Six was the only dog I ever loved. She came to me, smelling my hands, licking them warm. Sometimes I slipped her food meant for me. I felt shame. You couldn't name the animals. 'We need to get her out by the pines now, you hear,' he said. His voice was soft, he managed to blunt the edges sometimes. I stared at her all disjointed there, tufts of fur on the ground like plucked cotton. I rubbed her ears with my thumb. Vern reversed his truck, got out, scooped her up with a shovel and slammed her down on the metal. I couldn't believe his strength. The tattoo on his forearm wriggled as veins popped through the turquoise. He threw the shovel in beside her and looked at me. He always breathed heavy. A black-lunged wheeze.

'You gonna help me out, soft boy?' he said and bit down on his lip. I nodded and picked myself up. Climbed into the passenger seat. Raindrops on the windscreen had rivers in their bellies. We circled around to the back of the house. Soil churned under the wheels. The forest was vast. It went on and on like a brushstroke, like an echo. We drove fast along the edge and I felt my stomach tighten. Tree after tree after tree swept by us until it was a large animal. My mind formed cracks as sunlight skewered us through the gaps. Six's body shivered like she was still alive.

Vern pinched my neck as he drove. Tremors in his fingertips, like he was plugged into the mains. His thumb in circles over my skin. We drove past the house. Maw was inside. Jamie was out somewhere beating back the wild. Our last dog gone. We drove way out onto the asphalt. Past the school, the church, the library. Out into the open until he turned off by the water tower and onto a dirt road. Trees hid the sky. Pylons were posted throughout each field like stick men. Thin black wires connecting them. The wood had been burnt black by lightning and fires over time. Some were cut loose, impotent, erect and alone.

'Where we going?' I whispered. He pretended not to hear and pulled on the handbrake when there was no more road, when all there was, was musk seeping in from everywhere. You can always smell the wolf before it gets you. Vern's hands were the color of beets. His jaw visible under the skin, grinding. He didn't mind the dogs. When we stopped, he lit a smoke. Tossed the pack into my crotch. I took one out, rolled it between my fingers as he pinched the crest of his nose tightly.

'Help me get it done,' he said.

'Yessir,' I answered.

Six was heavy as a sack of flour. With my arms hooked under her hind legs, I stumbled and tripped, scared. My nose ran. Vern took us through the pines to a large sinkhole. He pretended he couldn't see me weeping, like he'd always pretend from that day on. His silence loud as thunder. We took her to the edge and he stopped, dropped her in. His cigarette burnt all the way up to his lips and the ash flaked off and got caught in his beard and eyebrows. Emerald eyes, a swamp in sunlight.

'This'll do,' he said and put his hand behind my head, holding the skull in place. He nudged her flank with the tip of his boot to make sure she went down and walked back to the truck. He shouted something as I stood observing my dog with her tongue hanging out slowly vanish. Another part of me taken by the woods, another good part. I thought I heard something in the distance. Thought I saw the shape of a man slide between the trees. But when I looked up there was nothing, just a wall of green. There and then not there.

Beat. Nothing. Beat.

'You need to give something back, too, you know,' said a voice behind my ear. 'It's the way of things. If you don't, we'll all be cursed. Wherever you go, it'll follow. Dog backwards is God,' he said, knocking a finger into the side of his head. When I looked down, I'd torn the cigarette to shreds.

Wings fanned the dust.

RAGNAROK

In Norway, the kids have been burning down churches. They wear death on their skin and paint their faces with white and black. Stripes across the eyes, down over the mouth. They bury clothes in the dirt. They are licked by night and bring the wild back in. There are a couple of tapes around town with the music those foreign kids listen to. Jamie bought them for nothing. Bands with names that looked like barbed wire and bramble weeds on the cover sleeve. Those tapes are his gospel. Jamie tries hard to feel Norwegian after dark.

Burnt-Mill cemetery is so quiet. Lungs curdle until all you are is silence. Soil bulges, uneven with roots. Jamie comes here when he wants to get lit. Everyone comes to get high in the evening. It is nat-ural, for some reason it is natural. He was drunk the other night. The jeering had made him sore. He has learned to hate everything at a dis-tance. Locked in a room behind his eyes, all meat hooks swinging. He figured out that if he sung to the dark, it would sing back.

Jamie's deformed legs, tooth-pick thin, almost boneless, haven't helped. He was born premature, in the early hours of a purple morn-ing. A difficult birth. Maw was cut open to get him out of her. Tugged out by the chin like a catfish. A huge pile of corncobs burned out-side. Old superstitions to prevent his entrance into the world. He was born into that cloud of smoke. Jamie's upper body developed normally enough. Bulked up in all the right places but his legs never grew right. They bowed outward. Flailed around when he ran fast, more cartilage than bone. The weakness in his walk meant the rest of him had to be like a mountain, his heart a volcano.

In the cemetery, the dead become calcium. They feed the

land, make the crops grow tall. At least they used to, before black stuff start-ed making folk unwell. Gave them vertigo. Gave them crawling sensa-tions on the skin and tingling in the fingers. The years of summer rain and warm damp made it spread wide. Once Jamie found a seashell in the graveyard. He loved to dig up buried things. The shell was some-thing that shouldn't have been there, like him. He lifted it up to his ear like a telephone and listened to all the voices inside. Over and over. There was a wolf living inside that seashell. Each time he lifted it up, the howl would crawl into his skull. Down into his guts. Finding it meant Harmswood was once at the bottom of a deep ocean, smothered in waves. He closed his eyes and the shadow of a whale swam over his head. The pines and conifers swayed in the current like black seaweed. In time, he forgot about the seashell but kept the wolf that lived inside it.

When they were still small, Blake told Jamie that he was a Vi-king. Whenever Maw brought men around, Blake took him upstairs, shut the door, and said his eye and Jamie's legs were marked by gods, that they were fated for something bigger and better than all of it. Jamie knows that this is a childish thing. But he holds onto the myth, holds onto the lie. On some level he believes, on some level he is not the bas-tard son of a whore, a drug-rat who tore up his mother and blinded his brother. On some level, there is greater meaning. Tiny seeds grow into ash-trees. But not tonight. Tonight is about feeling bad.

Huff Alley runs along behind Burnt-Mill. Crystal parapherna-lia, tin foil, and small syringes in the grass. Alcohol in hairspray cans that can be sucked clean out. This is the real Harmswood. Jamie never huffs, it's the line he's drawn in the sand. He can't bring himself to sink that low, not ready to go out like that. All one can hope for is a good death. At some point, he decided to turn fully nocturnal. Found it easier to pass out on H during the day and spend the nights wired on liquor, smashing out the truck windows in scrapyards. Spray painting obscenities on trailers and waiting for the sun to rise, for men to make the air blue.

A lot of the men died here in middle age. Outlived by their fathers and sons. Their hearts pulled the plug on them. Jamie passes graves so old that the ground has pushed coffins out like the body does shrapnel. The body always remembers. Ackermans made a name for themselves. The scrapyards grew emptier, the cattle all died, the crops were planted on the wrong side of the moon—but the woods went nowhere. He buried his jacket one night after a long walk down the asphalt. It was that walk that made him think too much. His brain grew large out there. Huge with no headlights to blot it out. No brown powder left. With his headphones strapped to his head, he dug and dug until his arms ached and his back burned. Stuffed it in there with all the world's calcium. There is a bald patch in the cemetery, sits like a disk under the sky. They call it the Devil's tramping ground. Legend goes he walks around in a circle thinking up new ways of tormenting people that are down on their luck. Jamie hoped that burying his jacket close to it would make him more Norwegian.

Whiskey splashes over his hands as he steadies himself. His lighter makes the tobacco sing. For a second, he feels a dull throb of sta-bility. The soil fills his fingernails. Soaks up its people. After Blake left, it tipped him closer to the edge. Left alone with the Devil, with God asleep in a deckchair—with nothing at all. The water tower is where he went with Blake that last summer. They climbed to the top, wet from the humidity, pink in the creases. It stank up top but the eastern breeze moved things along as they sat cross-legged. They shared a joint and then another as the sun fell.

Blew weed smoke out into the open air and watched it disperse. Blake said that in some cultures peopled be-lieved that the sun was eaten by a wolf each night and coughed back up in the morning. They pretended to howl over the fields through fits of laughter. Even then, Jamie felt that there was something in the water. Something bad eating up the crops, under their noses. His hand glides over the lettering of a gravestone as he pulls himself together. Fingers trace the sunken names. All meaning is packed into those names—it means thousands of things. It means nothing at all.

The jacket looks darker as he unearths it. At least, this is what he wants to see. His brother once told him that we see things as *we* are, not as *they* are. Always pulling quotes out of the nowhere. He brushes the words away, shakes the dirt off. Closer to being Norwegian. Pulls it over his shoulders, threads his arms through the sleeves. Throws his head back to gulp Jack Daniels like a river bird swallowing fish. He pushes the volume button all the way up and music stampedes over his eardrums. In the earthworm-heat, a calm comes over him. Behind his eyelids, a church with its roof on fire.

THE BALD-KNOB

She-wolf. Nothing on which she tramples can survive. She is said to live sometimes on earth, sometimes in the wind. The she-wolf can only bear cubs in thunder. Birth in thunder reminds us of the Devil.

Nothing on which she tramples can survive.

BLAKE

Maw had this nightmare whenever something went bad. She had it before every one of our dogs died. She had it before men left her and she had it before Jamie threw the stick into my left eye. It was the dream with Satan in the bathroom, sitting on the toilet. When Lead-Belly records came out, so did this dream. Men came and went throughout my childhood. Their voices crawled through the walls and sunk into the gravel outside. Ma's men. Over time, I became one of Ma's men too.

It was the same routine. They all drank, but not like her—they didn't change like Maw did. Her eyes narrowed with liquor and her tongue became a serrated whip. She shouted things in the middle of the night that scared them. They'd find her walking up and down the chicken wire fence in the yard, prowling and mumbling up at the trees. After a while, the men felt uneasy, thought that there was more than one person living inside my mother. While she talked, they were silent and smoked. She had a way of sniffing out weakness, the pink vulnerable parts. She would press on those parts, pierce them with words, drag the shame out into the room. I saw a lot of hard mountain men, proud whisky-barreled alligator men from all over Arkansas cave. I saw them leave in a line like our dead dogs with their tongues hanging out.

Maw lived out a fantasy with these people. She got under their fingernails like dirt. I heard her scoffing at them as they undressed. She made loggers feel like they carried twigs, farmers like they were children chasing pigeons. All they could do was yell and bang the furniture like apes, until she softened, submissive, making them hers again. I would slip my headphones on, open a book. In a town like Harmswood, people get so bored of themselves but Maw was nocturnal. Like my brother, like me, she wasn't the right kind of meat to be chewed up and swallowed. The three of us always got stuck in the town's teeth.

She used to tell me that the stars committed suicide out of loneliness. She saw herself in those stars. Sewn together with thin cords of cigarette smoke. A poem written in the mud by hooves, claws, and paw prints. I once told her that all people are full of stars, that stars are all full of people. That the particles of air we breathe are the same number as celestial bodies mapped out in space. Her eyes slid from ochre to ecru. She brushed away my words like mosquitoes. This is not how Maw saw the stars. She only saw herself—there and not there.

When a place is left to its own devices, it consumes itself. Spits out the pieces that can't be swallowed. With any patch of dirt, weeds will burst through the cracks. They will choke out cars and houses. Throughout my childhood, God was asleep. A fetus coiled under the blue-gray stones. He was burnt out of the fields with the rats. Left pieces of himself in the glint of fish scales, in the way deer turned their heads telepathically. After the accident, I buried God alive. I turned him into the eye I lost, planted him like a seed under the pines, the firs, the conifers. Maw kissed my face each time she looked at me. God was nowhere but in my blindness, and so I searched for him with my good eye closed. His absence was filled by the sound of animals fighting and we lived in the shadow of the sun.

Funny what stays in the end. What gets absorbed. Pinned to

the page like a dry butterfly. I could never imagine Maw or Vern as children. And yet all they were was infantile. Their past never allowed for the cleansing of old age, that slow dilution of self. What I did know about my granddaddy was enough to fill in the blanks. Maw still called him Sir when she drank.

Sir crawled out of two wars with the wires in his head hissing like cats. They never looked into things back then, how a father might eat his young. Maw and Vern had a connection that was formed out where stars kill themselves. While Sir was away, the twins were shuffled between relatives; they were each other's nest. In Norse myth, the giantess *Hel* was half corpse, part rotten. Growing up Maw was *Hel*. When I asked her about him, she was drunk enough to let the truth dribble out. My granddaddy was bad and all Ackermans came from that same kink in the chest.

'I don't believe in favorites,' she said one day in deep summer. My eye was sealed up with bandages, pus, and stitches. We were on the porch and she swatted the horseflies away when they landed on my face. She shook a cigarette out and pressed the nub up to her lips like a teat. Jamie sat with his back to us in the shade of a small fruit tree. I looked at the way his legs curved around under him. Maw wiped my eye clean, also looking.

'Sir loved me the more though,' she said with a little tilt in her voice. 'I was his pearly girly,' she said and drank. 'Till I got older and he didn't like that. Didn't like his meat too soft,' her mouth started doing that thing, that flexing like a mollusk. She squinted through the booze-film.

'The door would slam and all the leaves fell off the trees in one. The ground kind of sighed beneath him,' I loved it when Maw talked this way, even though it was painful. Her words held a type of magic—one of the things that made her too good for the cage she was born into. She needed me to listen and so she loved me. After the accident, my head was filled with her talking. She went on, knocking another cigarette out of the pack, lighting it with the stub of another.

'I always made sure Vern was outside. Pushed his butt out the window. I know he must have heard things through the plywood. Sir didn't even drink,' she paused to exhale. 'Came out of him pure,' she said.

I wondered what might have happened to Sir. The man before him and the man before that. Empty space is what I feel. That unknown gap in old maps that are filled in with spiny sea creatures. The older I got, the more I realized that everything that happened was his fault. We grew up in his ruins. I only ever saw one picture of my grandaddy. Some glassy shimmer in the eyes made him my mother's father. Eyes that did not belong to one person. He was smiling in the photograph, staring beyond the frame.

'I got thrown down the stairs for sleeping in late,' she said and tilted back the liquor. 'Walked with a cracked hipbone for two months. I couldn't stand straight but it was like nothing happened. He never remembered what he did,' she said. 'I heard him whimpering to himself at night, in that hour where dogs become wolves, he sounded itty-bitty small. I liked that,' she said quietly.

In the year before I was born, my grandaddy was found with his head blown off. Face down and butt-naked in the soil. Coyotes had chewed off his fingers and ran away with an ear. He left the cattle to Vern. To Ma, he left only memories. Sometimes she fixed me with a stare so deep like she wanted me gone, thrown out like soup bones. But no amount of hell would change the fact I came from inside her. That I was one of her little men.

When they came around in my youth, I pretended not to see, not to hear. That's what books are for, that's what a volume knob on your Walkman is for, that's what having a blind eye is for—not living the difficult things. As she got older, men paid in liquor or didn't pay at all. She said booze leveled her out, that it kept her mind from wriggling away. But I saw my reflection sliding around in those eyeballs. Before I left, the days were heavy as black birds on telephone wires. I was eighteen, choking for air when she lost the war to the other people in her head. Pills floated around in the toilet bowl after I graduated high school. That last summer, I helped her out of bed every morning. I bathed her and thought of all the filth of the town washed up in grey lye soap. We never did know who our fathers were. It never mattered. At night, I dabbed her forehead with a wet towel. The sound of trickling slowed her breathing right down, all that caught smoke. She made hamburger meat of her cheeks, chewing them free of dreams.

'I am half gone,' she said as I pulled my fingers through her hair. This was how it was with my mother; she would eat people and throw them up again. She would gorge herself and then go on hunger strike. She was a mouthpiece for their desires. They finished inside her and she charged double for the loss of life. Things got real bad after Maw was dumped by her longstanding regular. He came out of the woods to get lit at the tavern. She met him back there in the old days. From then on, she always took him in, no matter the state or stench of him. She liked that he could just as easily sleep in the gutter. Once he gave me a boar skull, pushed it straight into my hands, all ants and beetles, like I'd won something. I sensed things were wrong. She said a wretchedness was biting at her heels in the night. She said the trees were whispering again as I stroked her wet hair.

'Blakey, when I am all gone, leave me by the pines,' she said.

We never really know why we do the things we do. How a ripple becomes a wave. My only plan was to bolt fast until the trees got small. It happened one day out of nowhere. I'd been helping Vern load the trucks with cotton. Alongside the goats, he would work on the corn and cotton as a farm-hand. We had no money and he supported us with his G.I bill each month. It was just the two of us, burning out under the sun. Vern didn't want Jamie on the fields. Even though his upper body was stronger than mine. He didn't like the way my brother cut right through to the marrow. So he was somewhere else wandering around with hair swinging over his face. I turned around every now and then. Wished he was there so I could give him the finger and watch him go purple.

I was no good at it. Ma'd coddled me after the accident, didn't let me play outside anymore. She even took me out of school for a time and the house made my skin pale as a cave fish. But Vern needed me, like he had always needed me. At midday, we took a break and I fell into a pool of shade. He smirked, pulled two cigarettes out, and lit them with a match. He enjoyed standing above me—the shade was his shadow. We crouched down under the truck, leaning our backs against thick wheels, sweat pooled over our lips and stung our eyes—it felt like dying. The air caught fire and my uncle made a hissing sound between his teeth, his Adam's apple looked unnatural against the wide-open sky. He cleared his throat with words he couldn't say.

'You will kill her,' he said, keeping his gaze over the way. 'I know you're leaving us.' My stomach fell through me. Vern put the cigarette out on his tongue, shoved the roach in his pocket. 'It's a mistake,' he said. If a fly landed, it would have splintered me into pieces. I pressed myself hard against the vehicle, hoping that it would devour me, end me so that this feeling would also end. I screwed my eyes shut but the sweat still got in. Oxygen turned hard in my lungs. Nothing would come out as I tried to explain. My mouth moved and I felt the familiar vibration of my voice. The Bald-Knob rocked from side to side not knowing where to settle. He jabbed into my shame. Pulled it out, stringy and thin.

'Get us beer,' that's all Vern said, he wasn't really listening. He was thinking about things no one else knew. No one other than us. I got up and walked through the field towards the house.

'Dig deeper for the cold ones, boy,' he yelled. He never called me that, boy. It opened a divide, like I'd already left. The house creaked like it knew something was wrong. I went to the kitchen first for water. I needed water to loosen whatever it was that wouldn't let me breathe. The Bald-Knob hung back in the shadows. He was afraid of Ma. She'd be out back in her deck where I'd left her, feet stuck in a tub, scum from her soles floating to the surface.

Through the window, I watched Vern walk over to the pines. Saw him unbuckle his pants and piss with his back to the house, his head leant on the trunk. Bird shit slid down his left shoulder blade. I was too thirsty to think. When I turned on the faucet, it rattled and made a gurgling sound like a choking person was trapped down in the old pipes. It shook and spat out drafts of brown water slowly turning clear. I stared as it swirled down into the drain. Under my eyes, swallowed down into nothing. The sound of that dying little man in the drainpipe was why I left Harmswood for anything else that day.

I walked through the house and pushed the screen door open

with the tip of my shoe. She was there, staring right at me. She didn't blink. I knew which one was staring. I knew that soul, the vengeful one that wanted to see all the world burn. It emptied its ashtray in front of me and mumbled something. Into Ma's eyes grew a soft milky glow. I was her boy. Her little man.

'I had the dream again. The one where the air feels foul. Like I'm breathing in someone else's breath,' she said.

'Dreams are all lies, Maw,' I said.

'When you've been meeting with the Devil as long as I have, you know your worth,' she said. I stared at the end of her cigarette. She coughed and hit her chest. 'He's awful fat. Head all bald and shiny. He stops and grins at me,' she said. 'He laughs at me and everything is teeth, teeth, teeth.' Maw rolled her neck all the way around, clicking the vertebrae. She squinted.

'Just dreams, Maw, just dreams,' I said, not knowing how to leave her.

'Smells like fish when he opens up his legs. Calls me over to sit on him,' she said, moving her head side to side, disagreeing with herself. I hated this part, tried not to find meaning in any of it. The Bald-Knob spread his wing out stiffly. I saw him take a step forward in the corner of my eye. 'I never felt warmth like that. Too far down in the gutter for the sun,' she said. I wanted to take the others out of her one by one and feed them to the carrion bird.

'It's bad weather. It'll pass.' I said taking her hand. She pulled me in and stretched my damaged eye open with her fingertips, so that she could see all the blue-grey mess inside. She was always checking.

'Why must all us Ackermans have pieces missing?' she said.

Telling Maw I was leaving her was the hardest thing. So hard that a void howls where a memory should be. It has been torn out. All I have left is whatever it is that lives behind words. I only have glimpses, the flicking of a lighter with no spark.

'You'll leave me here with the dead. With the ghosts in the trees. You'll leave your Maw out here like a mutt,' she cried. The shame I feel cannot be digested by the Bald-Knob; it is too large, too alive still. 'Without you here, I'm all gone, you hear?' she said. She was frail, afraid all the time. The wrinkles around her mouth deepened. I kissed her forehead and it tasted bitter, citrus, powdery.

'It's just bad weather, Ma, it'll pass,' I said. She screamed into my body as I held her. It still rings in my chest. I ran upstairs and fumbled through my old books as she continued to curse and wail. They were in boxes limp, lifeless. I searched for Ovid but he'd seeped into the walls, crawled through the drains. I threw things together in a duffle-bag. Smelly sweaters. Jeans. My journals and other useless things. The records I left behind for my brother, the Walkman too. There was a bus out that evening. I'd already checked.

After I watched Vern down two beers, he drove me through town in silence. I asked a couple of folks but no one had seen sound nor sight of my brother. As we waited at the bus stop, my uncle just stood stiffly, shifting his weight and, then, he pushed a roll of dollar bills into my hand. He looked the other way as I climbed aboard. I was numb to him. My skin thickened. I sometimes thought about his goats for solace. I thought about how they disturbed and upset him. It was the last time I saw my mother. She had her first stroke three weeks after I left and then another two more years later that finished her. There and then not there. I stepped onto the Greyhound and my heart called out for Jamie one last time. The trees got smaller and smaller. I tried to forget the backwoods. How the country's secrets were all tarred and feathered.

The Bald-Knob spread his wing.

He took a step forward.

It was my last summer of black sunlight.

Part II.

Ergot, Sanctus Ignis.

SCREECH-OWL

There was once a woman who ran up into the mountains and there was changed into a bird. As often as she was killed, the bird became multiplied. The only way to avert catastrophe was to kill a member of the species in whose veins the tide of life ran strong. All sacrifices were but one and the same. She was still alive and incarnate in all the birds of existence.

CUSTER

The Osage Indians used howls to drive out white settlers from the Ozarks. They were six feet tall and bred fear down into the valleys. They darkened their faces with plant juice. Around the eyes, across the mouth, like the tattooed Scottish Picts with their blue swirling dragons. The Osage would slither around a campfire, hissing and hooting, tapping their weapons on stones, thumping the earth—a dance of antlers through lunar teeth. The mountain echoed with their voices and wept as all mountains do. Custer has a secret. He keeps it hidden inside flames.

People of the distant fires. That is what he's managed to scrape out of the hard earth of his past. One translation of the many, after years of searching for something to call his heritage. But where was the rest of him. What was the Seminole name he was given by his mother before they took him and his sister away? Before the residential school stripped them bare. He can't remember his mother's voice, electrocuted out of him over and over again through the hellish years where torture was met with a wall of silence. A castration. Made to sit on a stool in the school corridor. A cone-shaped paper cap balanced on his head. Not allowed to move. Not allowed to make a sound. The word 'DUNCE' written across it in tall capitals. It was too late when he learned the meaning of that word. Always too late.

The nuns were cruel. Cruel to them all. Cruel in a way that their faith demanded. As if it wasn't really them that was doing those unspeakable things. They made the children drink cod-liver oil when they spoke their language until they puked up their native tongues. He was given a Catholic name, branded like livestock. Made to repeat this new name until the word was a burning coal. Too hot and painful for a child's mouth to contain. Slowly he would forget. Forget himself. Forget his bloodline. But Custer spat the coal out each time. He bolted. Starved himself. Thin enough to slip through the smallest gaps and run with the foxes, fly with the night-birds. He heard something calling to him from beyond the cold stone walls. A hiss, a hoot, a yip. The Osage cut themselves before they left. They bled their spirit into the earth, the wind, and the pines. Panther-blood. Wolf-body. He wanted it to be real. Needed it to be true.

The school was hidden. Even from God. After lights out, Custer would drop three feet to the ground and twist his skinny ankles each time. He'd run through the small trees until they became tall. Following that sound, that whistle, the rustling up ahead. His feet and hands were cut up, his yellow lice-ridden nightgown torn and shredded as he pushed in deeper. Naked, freed. Deeper into anywhere else. Deeper, wilder until not even the moon could see him running. One of the others would tell on him to avoid a beating. Someone always caught and dragged him back. Until he plucked up the courage to do it again. He always forgave the children that snitched.

Once he tripped up and battered his temple on a wet stone.

All went black, but he listened to the water as it trickled from behind, under him, soothing his guts and running down into the deep well of a sinkhole. The wound let the air out of his skull, relief. He heard the sighs and wails of ghosts fleeing, carrying his soul with them. A deep shade of red expanded behind his eyelids, red sky falling over black-tipped mountains, a vision like the ancients had. For the first time since capture, he felt protected. He wanted to let the water wash him away, to take him through that hole in the ground.

They called it killing the Indian and saving the man. Being who you were in that place was the greatest sin of all. He woke up back inside. Whipped again, beaten again, starved. None of it could touch him after he felt earth's cradle. In the coming years, he took other kids back out there, tried to show them the same vision. The hole in the ground became a place they went to bury parts of themselves and whisper their pain into the soil, to give their spirit away for safekeeping. He told them that their hair would grow back slowly, that new shoots of language would sprout where their tongues were pulled out. No rods, fists, or fish oil maimed him in the way it did the others, who creased up into themselves like burning paper tigers. As long as his heart was buried there under the pines, he could withstand it all.

SCREECH OWL

He knows that all the gods are broken.

Even before the boy.

Even before the end.

He knows.

CUSTER

It was a strange thing they demanded. These gods. An uncomfortable thing. As a child, Custer had learned to eat off the ground whenever he escaped. Roots, frogs, and bird's eggs. Scooped snails from their shells. Sometimes he would be out there for days trying to get closer to the mountain. Find his way into one of the cave systems. Some of it made him so ill he could have died. The wrong fungus. Curled up and shivering, drying out like tobacco. Until he found the right fruit. It gave him new eyes. He saw all the gods lurking, up in the pines staring back. The trees were full of them. Huddled together, skinny and fierce. Yellow teeth bared, they looked like him in his animal side, darker, heavy-jawed. They spoke through the eyes and clicked their tongues. He told no one of this, until after Vietnam.

They gave him a Purple Heart for his legs. When they caught him and hacked them off, time ran away like a scared elk. Somehow, he had not died. The paradise of wind in the leaves kept the fire burning inside—deep, deep down a heart pumped blood beneath the earth. He was sure it was his time to be carried out of his body by the birds, reborn in the larvae of blowflies. Somewhere out of the dark, he heard two pearly notes. A screech owl called, threading him into the great pine-sea of the Ozarks and so he crawled back. Tied knots around his bleeding stumps. Pulled his body through the mud back to camp and dragged his dead partner with him. G.I.s were merely another link in the chain of warriors. Playing-cards and packs of Lucky Strike cigarettes like little Japanese flags—all poems to tuck inside the armor. Things they needed with them at the end, after seeing what they saw. After seeing a person twisted, already mummified, legs and torsos along riverbanks, trenches and tree lines. Small children haggling for brown balls of dope from empty film canisters. Brothers offered up their sisters with sunken eyes and crow's feet. The war brought out a kind of sick love in the enemy.

He drank the mud. Sipped the dew off leaves. The gods followed him as he crawled. His fingers pushed into the earth. The corpse of his companion felt like it was pushing into him, as if one had to absorb the other. A patrol found him and kicked the gods away. Custer remembers opium, he remembers velvet moth wings, losing himself in the eye of them. The dead hillbilly partner was sent back to his hometown in a plain wooden box, cocooned in a flag. Custer sees the man dancing to machine-gun fire every time he closes his eyes. When he was brought back to Harmswood, he bought up a disused gas station. He wanted to own something that for once couldn't be stripped away. He never forgot the god's hunger. Never forgot how he was spared twice. How he had to give something back.

Deer-season was the right time. Antler is tough to penetrate. To wear on the face. But it makes good for hiding once done. Antler mask and pelt from the buzzards. Black feathers in the night make you invisible. Two men have always helped Custer with the work. They are loyal. Survivors of the school like him. Survivors because they kept it buried. They are younger and stronger. Their blood goes back, deep into the soil's memory, deep into the wolf's mind. One came back from Missouri and collected scrap metal from all over town. The other was axe throwing champion five years in a row in Oklahoma and always looked for ashwood to make bows for shooting. They are silent men and work well with their hands in the dark. They came back for Custer when he bought the gas station and have been part of the cycle since. The only two that didn't burn up like paper tigers. When they were children, they screamed into that hole in the ground. Custer made all the school's children howl like a wolf pack before they were found and dragged away.

    He is old now; it will be his last offering. A tribute for all of those slaughtered. For all of those needlessly taken from mothers and homes. Needlessly driven to madness and despair and calamity. The nuns separated girls from the boys and the priest took it upon himself to cleanse his sister with the Holy Spirit. He said it flowed through him like a fountain. A bridge between this world and God's. She had physicals each week, checking to see if she was still a virgin. 'You better come back here with everything you left,' he would say in a voice full of goat's hooves. The girls were then sent fruit picking in the afternoons and the mud of his voice cracked inside them. The Holy Spirit seeped out in spider's silk trails as they walked under those small trees. Little Deer was her Seminole name, this Custer never forgot.

    In the fall, he sees his sister at the edge of the forest. Night after night. The war he fought tangled his wires. He sits out back watching for her to appear walking along the tree line. One day he will join, he will go back in and dig for his heart. He will be there to protect her. She had gotten it worse than him inside. Little Deer pushed against the pain until she became one with it. She was found in a bathroom stall, soaked in her own blood, wrists cut clumsily. They called her sick, a born sinner, and buried her the next morning in an unmarked grave before the sun was in the sky. Custer can't remember where they put her but knows she is inside every screech owl.

Harmswood was founded somewhere between the blade's cut and the musket's fizzle. A sleepless fear dribbled down through the line of ancestors. It has always been lurking. The Osage were finally put down. Domesticated, tricked and killed off one at a time for a fortune of minerals. After that, it was moonshiners that hollered to scare people off of their stills. They called it Sasquatch, they called it the Ozark Howler. A large black cat, a moose with wings and a human voice—a hissing, gurgling sound that carried over from the pines to the fringes of the town. Voices on the wind, large and damaged. The sound went back centuries. America was a foreign land, even to itself. A theatre of white-toothed grins, headache-green lawns, picket fences fitted to impale. Out on the other side of the TV screen. Those pretty folk only came down to the nature-state for monsters.

The children still wet themselves. Winter comes and footprints in the snow aren't wolf or coyote or feral pig. Too many toes, too familiar. Devils' feet, farmers call them. The old spirits ran in circles chasing each other, forgetting themselves in the mist. So long-forgotten, crossed off the map by the new God. It was hard to find them but Custer managed. He found the gods hiding up in the caves, picking fleas out of each other's fur. He knew how to please them. No matter how much things changed in the town under the Teeth, the specters went nowhere. Nothing ever really died. It never really ended, somewhere the same person was being born over and over again, living out the same nightmare over and over. Blood and thunder, snakes under stones, the world kept turning. Hunters kept their eyes fixed on a fire so that the dead didn't drag them back. When Custer could look no longer, an owl screeched three times over the acres.

The gods were hungry, especially for certain children. Through surviving his own childhood, Custer learned that the color white is pain. White crosses, dog-collars, the milky diaphanous white of the Holy Spirit. Turkey-wattle white of small men. White is a lie that contains everything and nothing at all. It is a trickster color that silences as snow that falls to conceal the tracks of predators. It harbors fire and ice. Both burn things alive.

CHICKEN LEGS

The man with no legs ran the gas station for as long as Jamie could remember. Half native. Most days he'd be sitting outside in a wheelchair, smoke billowing out his nostrils, his hair long and heavy like a horse's tail. Jamie decided to be a dropout very early. He grew sick of the aching ribs and bruised balls. The yellow hum of concussions. His name thrown around like a curse word. The medieval freak show never went away. One day, he stopped by to ask Custer for cigarettes and lighter fluid—he was heading out to the woods. Bull gone. Blake gone. He hoped never to return. Custer maneuvered himself over the little step of the entrance and around the counter. His face bore elephantine wrinkles, hanging loose from the bone. In the grey morning light, everything was waking up in the same way that photographs are almost alive. Dust swirled in beams of sunlight when he opened up a drawer.

Jamie watched those searching hands and they loosened up a knot in his chest. He became featherlight as his eyes scanned the space, darting from soda cans in the refrigerator, to fishing rods lodged above his head, through the ceiling like spears. Tingling as a grunt drew his gaze down to the pack of smokes in Custer's palm. A small hand-poked tattoo of a snake coiled round an egg on the man's forefinger. As Jamie let a bunch of quarters drop to the counter, Custer grasped his hand and pulled him in close.

No words came, his voice had leapt from his throat like a frog to hide beneath some lily pad. Some soft force held him there. A heat swelled between them. Jamie's gaze dropped down to a curved pipe poking out of the slit in Custer's shirt and then to an exposed colostomy bag. He felt stupid, embarrassed, but Custer wouldn't let go of his hand. He shook his head side to side. Numbed out by the soft, strong heat.

'It's no small thing living inside a shadow,' Custer said and let go, leaning back and interlacing his fingers. The heat washed over Jamie's body like a wave of wings beating and made the frail glass door rattle on its hinges. Jamie looked down at his palm, at the cigarettes, at the man with no legs. A sense of urgency came over him. Of needing to tell someone before he disappeared. Before the H burned him from the crops like vermin.

'I'm heading for the pines. Don't figure I'll be coming back,' he said. A pause as Custer started rolling from his own uncut tobacco. He observed the way Jamie held his sleeves tightly over his arms, the way he smelt bad, the way the sole from one of his sneakers was loose and flapping.

'You might see things in there. Things that come out when they're hungry,' he said and wheeled out from behind the counter.

Jamie thought about school, about boys sneaking peeks at pornography, burning the corners of a desk with lighters, shooting spitballs into girls' hair. He thought about how he was missing out on nothing, nothing at all. There were a few people left in Harmswood that were like Custer. Natives weren't talked about. Jamie had never spared a thought for them. They were always closer to shade. They helped out loggers and worked construction, half-smoked cigarettes tucked behind their ears, baseball caps and cheekbones that sliced the wind wide open. The children they had were given white names. Jamie was pretty sure that the nickname Custer was someone's boneheaded joke.

At school, teachers treated him like something between an

invalid and a criminal. Truth just beyond his fingertips, a foreign country. His mind always swarmed like bats, manically weaving. In that moment, when he felt heat pass from one pair of hands to another, when Custer mentioned shadows, Jamie felt himself move an inch closer to the pale blue pool of his brother's eye. Carried through the air from bed to forest floor. Something familiar, something known to him. Custer's cigarette was long and cone-shaped and packed to the brim. Square hands delicately filled and folded the rolling paper. He lit both of their smokes with a match cradling the flame in his hand. They inhaled, watching the road and the field beyond burn where a harvester hung its head. The guard dog's chain tinkled as it came to rest on the stumps of its master. It yawned and its gums were black and pink. Jamie's lungs were on fire.

'I think God's dead,' said Jamie. 'Or just a regular bum. A waste of everyone's time.'

'There is a door in the forest where we put our hearts, all of our pain, as children,' said Custer. Jamie glanced at the tattooed finger, the little blue snake wriggled.

'You mean the old sinkhole?' asked Jamie his bones filling with storm clouds. Custer continued.

'I've been going out there since forever ago. It only gets wider. The loneliest moon fell from the heavens into the Ozarks. Inside, it is a nest built from the hearts of those who have already died once,' he said and inhaled.

Blake had told Jamie that Pluto was both a planet and a god. The same size as its closest moon. How there was double meaning in all things. It clung to him like a leech, this sphere with a skewed orbit.

Blake said there were worlds within worlds, some couldn't be seen with the naked eye. Some were so far up, others deep down under. One thing could easily be something else. The smoke made his brother's voice linger in the air like it was coming out of the dog's mouth each time it yawned.

'Why're you telling me this?' Jamie asked.

'My Mama was raped in the Everglades by a white man and that's how I was made. Me and my little sister. She came up here from the swamps with us to get away from the man that helped create us.' He took a deep drag and let smoke flow.

'We were on a reservation up north. They took us in the night. Took my sister and beat me hard when I fought back. Gave me this pretty thing,' he pulled his fringe back to reveal an ugly welt over his eyebrow. Horseshoe-shaped.

'Then Residential School took something and then Nam. Everything comes back for you in the end,' he said. 'Everything.'

Jamie's heart started to beat faster. In a way, he hadn't felt since that year with Bull. Before H became his world. Before Blake took off. His wolves shook their fur dry, sniffing at Custer's words. They howled and lost themselves in the echo. It was good to know that there was something hiding in the soil, that the wind in the pines knew it. A truth that rustled through the tall grass stalking him. There was so much more he had seen when he was still too young to fight. The cloud of it hung heavy. Everyone knew about the haunted school. Kids went out there looking for the man who walked out of the mines and slept in the pines. The floors were littered with glass pipes, beer cans, crushed tins of hairspray, underwear, leaky condoms. No one said a word about what happened there in the dark. Something in the crackling burn made Jamie feel close to this man. That, somehow, they shared a nest. He pictured Custer as a small child running. Feet on leaves. He pictured himself, his brother, and that other thing. He smelled his skin as the ember reached his fingers. He looked down before letting it fall. The dog whined. Beneath the tongue, the teeth, the breath was the same as his. Without realizing, he was staring at Custer's uneven stumps.

'Bad butchers,' he said. 'I survived the school just in time to be shipped off to a hell on the other side of the world. Shoved a hundred rounds of M60 ammo and a mortar into my hands. Gave me a hillbilly partner who had a mongoose for a pet. Homer, he called it. They liked us for trackers, said that we had the nose for it. It's different bush out there, everything's a little wetter, a little closer. We were pathfinders,' he said.

'Third day in the jungle, my partner spotted a trip wire caught in the dew. The mongoose was hanging over his shoulders the whole time, nibbling his earlobes, whispering instructions. To me, it just looked like a cobweb. In a moment, it was over. They were in the trees, you see. Hunting us the whole time. The first slug went clean through his throat. He stumbled back with his arms out like a human shield. I watched him dance, his hands and feet shaking. Split open,' he said. 'I never did see where Homer went,' he said.

'You were hit?' said Jamie.

'Both knees shot through, limp as dead rabbits. One slug in the gut. But that wasn't enough. They crawled down through the leaves, with their knives and hatchets. Boys your age and younger with nothing behind the eyes. I heard water over my cracking bones,' he said.

'Whenever I close my eyes, I see that man dancing,' he said and put his hand on Jamie's arm.

'They cut our hair and gutted out our language,' said Custer, staring out over the open ground. 'The sinkhole was for those of us whose hearts had grown bones. Everything bad that happened we threw into that great open mouth,' he said taking his hand again. 'We're all cripples here'. For the first time in his life since the accident, Jamie felt held between an old man's palms.

CUSTER

A gecko crawls up the wall. One padded foot glides out in front of the other. Eyes licked clean by a fat tongue. Custer wonders what this little creature has in store for it today, whether it will even survive. Beams hit the glass. The light touches each object and comes to rest on his forehead. That time in the morning where night retracts her claws is when one thing becomes another. If there is anything Custer has learned, it is that misinterpretations are beautiful. The children who died come back as lizards, as birds, as fish. As stone's memory, as river's wisdom. Half-heard. Half-seen.

The gecko whips its tail and disappears into a crack. Custer rolls out of bed. He pulls himself into the wheelchair, swings the colostomy bag under his arm, and pushes the foldout mattress up against a weak plywood wall. It is too early to open up and he sits enjoying the empty space, the murmuring fridges, the endless tinnitus. Nothing is ever completely without song. He tugs the chord of the ceiling fan. This has been his life since the war, watching the spirits of small things grow and falter. The buzzard is the only animal that goes nowhere, he stays always with his people, does what no one else has the stomach to do.

The dog barks outside. He wheels through the aisles with a notepad, checking off stock. Sodas and cigarettes are getting low, flies for the fishermen need to be ordered in before the month is out. Custer's is the first checkpoint in and out of town. Other natives hang out there, too. Constructions workers, loggers, drunks all come around. Every night, they come around. A couple of generations hungry for the lost people's secrets. The door handle rattles and a voice hollers his name. Splitting open in the morning quiet. He wheels over, unlocks, opens up, and Crowbar is in his doorway. An old trapper. He shuffles in with a bent spine. Custer backs up, all the way until he reaches the counter. The dog cries.

Giving trappers their liquor when they come back from the wilds is a ritual, a duty. Their clothes stink of fire and rain, stained with moss and critter's gore. Their eyes glisten with all the colors in birdsong. Crowbar's stare is moonless. He comes from a long line of fur trappers. Hunts predators. Mainly keeps wolves off the flatland. They'd become a problem years back, came down from the Teeth after they were reintroduced further north. Trappers had their own ways up there. Their own myths and superstitions. Starlight can't shimmer off plywood the same way it does off pine needles.

Custer pulls out a bottle of brown liquor from a drawer beneath the counter. Pours two fingers of it into a coffee mug and offers it up. Crowbar gulps down the sting. His body reeks. Too many months out there, too many nights where sleep doesn't come easy. He downs a second and heaves a busted trap onto the counter, it clatters making the whole frame shake. The ugly thing is bent all the way back so that the coils bulge. Mangled and deformed. The trapper breathes in like an ox after his second drink. Heavy in the throat.

'You looking to buy parts?' says Custer. He leans in as if to smell the steel. Small dents run all the way up and down like fingernails in clay. He can only see them because the light is right, because the day it not yet fully formed. A feeling flutters in his chest, a little bird flitting from rib to rib.

'I know of nothing with the brains to take a bear trap apart,' says Crowbar. 'We were up there shooting whitetail. Laid down a couple of these in case of panthers,' he says. Custer sees antlers peeking

They said the trees talked. Down the line. Hunters through the ages with bunches of wild geese tied to their sides, beaver pelts, and elk antlers as crowns. They all went mad and drank and forgot their madness. They all saw things. They all thought they saw things. Every farmer's fantasy was to see the world as the hunter did. As they milked diaphanous udders, as they climbed into the tractor with the sharp sting of a hemorrhoid. They dreamt of the hunter and carved grooves into the soil. Wishing to feel the lips of a paw-print some day.

'Go to sleep, friend,' says Custer. Crowbar looks up and they hold each other in a gaze. Sometimes, no words can catch the truth. The trapper turns and moves through the store like a boy spanked. Deflated. Shamed. He takes the last six-pack and a cigarette carton under his arm. Before leaving, he stops, swelling with the last of his embers. Gets close to Custer's face.

'Never forget who made you, red-man,' he says leaning over the wheelchair. Custer doesn't react as he turns to leave. Dogs will bark for a reason. Dogs and children sense the invisible. Outside, he sparks a match. The smoke plumes. He wheels on past the irrigation pumps, the elephant-trunk machinery. A mass of pipes leans against the wall, cobwebs woven into tapestries that connect one object to another. The land around the gas station is a dumping ground. Folks leave farming equipment on his lot during winter's drinking months. The land stretches out for a couple of hundred feet before the first few saplings start thickening the eye.

At the far end, there is a small shed. Inside the shed, three wooden racks are lined up. Draped with layers of rye, like saddlebags, still moist, shimmering with dew. They need to stay hanging until the air has dried out every last drop. Long brown stems, drenched. Custer pinches the end of one and tilts it sideways so that the liquid thickly slides. He brings it up to his nostrils and sniffs. He thinks of the old trapper traumatized by all the worlds prowling alongside this one. Frail as one of his contraptions. He lets go of the plant.

Two large cedar-wood tables sit in the middle of the space and, on each, piles of bones have been arranged. Bones pulled from the earth around the school. His brothers and sisters. Bowls with pestles inside them. Feathered skins hang from hooks on the wall. Bone and skin are kept but flesh is given back. Nothing left alive to clean up the dead. One thing he knows about his lost people is that the birds are sacred. They get the dead to where they need to be. They tear the soul from the body and the screech owl makes sure we never forget. This is his heritage. Scale beneath murk, a slit pupil, cranes severing the air. The rest he has built through the pain of loss. He takes out another paper, fills it with tobacco and sprinkles a pinch of bone-powder over it like a light frost.

He pulls in deep, letting the snake unwind inside him. In that shed, he is a God like the small gecko. Sometimes he knows he is losing his mind and likes to watch it unravel from afar. The whispers, unseen and everywhere. Such a thin line between curse and blessing—spider's saliva caught in sunlight. 'Fear isn't pointless,' he says to himself and hums a deep wooden drone. That one tune is all that's left from his childhood before the residential school. All of it, locked up inside that single hollow note. He smokes and paradise is a birdcage. Paradise is an alligator slumbering into a yard, dragging its claws over the wooden porch. Paradise is a higher truth, the animal scratching at your door. Even before the boy, he knew that the gods were all broken.

Tap. Tap. Tap.

Fingers drum the wood.

THE CUT

Blake said memory was Odin's second crow and Jamie wonders if that's all he is to his brother now—a memory. Out in open ground, every time a fox coughed, it bent the brain a little. The smell of itchy blankets is behind him. The smell of Blake, the smell of Bull and of sizzling brown powder in a spoon. His big brother read to keep the world at a distance but that was never Jamie. Dusk was his way. Owls swiveling their heads and foxes coughing that shatter the air like glass. He hurries, huddled under telephone cables. The streetlight flickers. Eyes water from the smoke in his lips. Custer's cut gave him dreams. His thoughts are all sculptures that ripple in wind. It was a better way. The best way he found to stay alive. A soldier turned feral by war. War is what cracks the brain. Everyone has their own reason for being eaten alive. He never told a soul about seeing Vern as a woman. It didn't feel right to talk about what he did at night.

Custer had a better way than all the rest. He had a cripple's way. The truest things about Harmswood are asleep in those pines. He has always eaten the fruit. Even as a child, he took a liking to it. Maw used to collect it secretly from the tree line and knead it into the bread, sprinkle it over the meat as seasoning. Raw, fresh, sprouting from the ground, spread through the rye. A fungus that flared up through the trees and grew where the ground was moist, on either side of the creek. Jamie kicked H after Custer gave him the cut to smoke. He said that all memory is a song soaked into the soil, the bark, the stones. There were more things Custer made him do, more than just eating and smoking the cut.

Turquoise powder had burned its way through the best part of a decade. The worst thing for the town since the mines shut down. After the buzzards died off, Custer was fixed on the idea that man needed to take on the role of the vulture. 'We need to bury them. We need do for them what they've always done for us,' Custer said. This was Jamie's first chore. He brought all the dead birds back that had fallen from the pylons and buried them in mass grave a few hundred feet behind the gas station. It was slow work. There were always fresh ones out on the asphalt. Jamie searches for the dead, high on the cut. Each buzzard has a story. In that haze, he turns them inside out. Everything under the skin is a deep shade of red. Once he picked one up and the skeleton of a viper fell out of it. He spots one about a day old. Opens up the garbage bag to swallow the body. Picks it up by the foot and ants topple out of it. He takes a drag and blows smoke into the buzzard's face and the beak opens. In his delirium the bird appears to spill ev-erywhere like tar, the ants wail up at him in a chorus. A fly lands on his cheek and Jamie thinks he might collapse into dust from the force of it. He thinks about the accident sometimes when high. Unlike H, Custer's cut makes the whole world swell, glow, and billow. He thinks about how it was instant. How his brother fell back crying. How man and beast are one and the same.

It felt good be part of the process. Included in the ritual. Jamie'd been going out there for years in the dark with a sleeping bag, a flashlight, and a Walkman. It was good to know that the blackest of feelings could also be the truest. Through that truth, he developed a loyalty to Custer, through the time spent in haunted schools. He understood the world not in objects, but for what lived inside those objects. For the life blown into them from beyond. He hits the side of his flashlight again and again so that it won't die. The best time to gather is when the sun fades. He keeps walking. Down over the hill towards Cleaver's tavern.

Two lights hover over the doorway and a sleeping bloodhound outside breathes in the dust. Cleaver's is a watering hole for any trucker passing through. Jamie stays on the other side of the road. The locals all know who he is in there. It was Ma's bar in the old days. Nearly all her men came lit from Cleaver's.

Would it all end if there was no place like this? If it was ashes? He turns the flashlight off. The bloodhound looks up. Ears go back, teeth and wrinkles. It barks once and growls. Would it be different if predators had nowhere to drink? He turns the light back on and it flickers over the road, turning his thin form into a yeti. He puts his hands up and arches them. Pushes his shoulders up next to his head. 'This is what isn't,' he thinks to himself and tilts the light in a way that makes his shadow longer so that it stretches out all the way to the next town and the town after it. The more he tilts, the more it stretches until the land is covered in him. A trick of the light has turned him into a Goliath, the biggest he's ever felt. Perhaps that's all God is; a trick of the light.

Another deep bark. Something watches from the tall grass as it always does. Another trick of the light. There haven't been wolves about for a time. But something has been ripping the goats open. Eating the heart and leaving the rest. Something older than time watches him from that tall grass. Vern neglects his goats and Maw slips into the next realm. Jamie watches his shadow stretch out into space. That ancient thing watches him, bloated with hearts and voice boxes.

Two men walk out of the bar. Moonshiners. Faces swollen. No one knows exactly where the stills are in the mountain. They guard them like dragons. Some said that all myths in the Ozarks was just a bunch of moonshiners making noise to scare folk from their stills. They spot Jamie dancing with his shadow. The bastard boy with chicken legs. They look at each other and one puts a finger to his lips as the other edges closer to the bloodhound, takes the leash into his hands. Finger-man sways on his feet, head tilted back. As Jamie twirls around in the darkness, like oil in water, Dog-man puffs spittle through his nose, elated. 'Oh, man,' he says in a hushed high-pitched voice. 'Oh, man, he gonna get it.' The finger-man puts thumb and middle to his mouth and whistles like an arrow through the air that hits Jamie, skewers him to the spot. Everything stops. Time, his heart, everything. Still with his back to them and the flashlight flickering. He knows. Knows he should've kept walking.

There is silence and a claw rips the velvet. Light bleeding in from the other side could be a star, a pearl, or a little death. Jamie turns around, sees them both staring at him. Dog-man coils the bloodhound's leash around his arms as the animal jolts trying to spring free, barking. Jamie does not hear it, just watches. Everything slows. Finger-man lowers his hand down from the mouth. Everything slows. They will make him run. Run until even the moon can't see him running. It all rushes in, from every direction. Everything slows.

'Oh, man. Oh, man, he gonna get it. You gonna rip him, ain't you boy? Rip him up,' says dog-man, slapping his hound on the flanks—getting him battle-ready. Finger-man is a boy really, a weathered boy. Jamie feels like he knows him, like he could tell his voice through a wall. Perhaps together, perhaps apart. Perhaps they've come around the house. Or is it Bull? It can't be Bull. Finger-boy speaks.

'Think you better run, child. Think you better fly,' he says and his voice is on all fours—pulling itself across the asphalt. He has a couple of heartbeats before the world splits open. So, he runs. Drops the bag of dead birds. He heaves his pelvis this way and that, throwing his legs around like oars. Jumps over a rut in a field, feet meet the soil. Bloodhounds are silent when they run. The flashlight is a chaos all its own. His foot hits a rock and he clatters, sprawling like a birthed foal, all limbs and no center. The flashlight rolls away. The bloodhound is nowhere. Jamie pushes himself up and the world is waves. He grabs for the flashlight. It could be moments, it could be years—it could simply be now, now, now.

As the beam flickers, something shines back. Not stars, not pearls, not little deaths. Paws pad the soil. The last handful of cows are there, survivors. Staring back through space. The dying light catches in their eyes. Jamie turns it off and then on again. When he squints, they are alligators. Submerged in a sea of wet grass, still silent, waiting for something to fall their way. He turns it off again, waits. The dog is somewhere coming for him, but not yet. He turns it on. The alligators are now children with bags over their heads, holding candles, hogtied. Jamie can still feel a part of him running deeper into that field, the part that never fell. The children are motionless, different shapes and sizes. Ghosts, cows, alligators. They are more than one thing.

The battery has died. It may not be the bloodhound; it may be what's been stalking him his entire life. It may be one of them. A wet nose between his legs, a rough tongue. Paws pad the soil. The bloodhound is whimpering, backing away. He must burn it all down and make use of the ashes.

SCREECH OWL

Pluto has five bestial moons:

The first is Kerberos – A three-headed mongrel that guards the underworld, just out of sight.

The second is Hydra – a nine-headed serpent who when beheaded sprouts two more heads. Icy, glacial.

The third is Styx – the slow death-river with its soft tongue flowering over everything and everyone.

Charon the boatman is the same size as Pluto and looks for coins under soft tongues.

Last there's Nix: the night, our mother.

CUSTER

'There are wolves and then there is everything else,' Custer says. 'Are you a wolf or are you nothing?' A large bowl in his lap, dark liquid glistens in the moonbeams. The constant flick of a zippo lighter. It is the long bone of winter now. The boy came back to him in the end. As always. He came over and over again after the first time and Custer gave him work to do. Small things at first. Collecting the dead buzzards. Then more. The boy came back after years of being hunted. So, he took the cripple in and out into the night with Missouri and Oklahoma. They silently push his wheelchair over the soil. The boy seems calm. Calmer than expected. He was no stranger to ruined schools and sinkholes.

'We are seers. We know that nothing is what it seems,' Custer says, his breath is clouds. The boy looks curious but haggard and thin. Devours each word. They paint his face bone-white from the nose up. A black line running down the middle, splitting him in two halves, seen and unseen. Oklahoma and Missouri do this while Custer keeps talking. 'This is Asi,' he says, bringing the bowl closer to Jamie's lips, the smell rich and pungent, like many tea-leaves congealed and left to ferment in dark places. He'd been giving the boy some of his cut to smoke, slowly blended to wean him off of his obvious junk problem. To clean him out. Custer upped the dosage a little more each time and made sure that the sight sustained him.

'We make it from what you smoke, but purer. Connects the seer to the fire inside. The Seminole have always taken it to summon the shouter, the master of breath— the one that put the howl inside the wolf,' he says. Before they drink, Custer pulls out three stalks of rye from under the seat of his wheelchair. Slowly, he picks off the black magic that has grown all the way up them and crumbles it into the bowl. When all three stalks are bare, they bring it to the boy's lips and then sip it themselves. It hits the little punching bag at the back of the throat.

'No matter who you are, no matter where you come from—a man will always be full of the shadows that haunt him. You are no one as the earth is no one,' says Custer through a mudslide. Jamie splutters and wretches. Hands hold his head, squeeze his cheeks for the mouth to open like making a calf drink milk from its mother's udder. Body of Christ, blood of Christ, soil, earth, the pain of truth all enter him and the cripple's mind bleeds out into the all.

Unblinking specters. Echoes of birds in the skull. The flame of a lighter, fireflies, cigarettes come together like the sun beating down. The boy saw his wolves in the long hours that followed. Some asleep, others chasing each other into the deep with squeals and yelps. Others sitting up straight to guard him—it is the first time he's seen what they looked like, the seashell-wolves he keeps inside. With them close, he settles his head down into a pillow of pine needles. Custer's purpose was to give voice back to those who were silenced. He pulled their soul from the carcass and made the world see it in the light of distant fires.

Something crashed in the treetops. Custer led them in a broken language. He built his story. He made choices and had no way of knowing his true lineage. Too young when they took him, broke him, skinned him alive. Jamie also knows that this doesn't matter, that if you find something that speaks to you through that darkness, brings your nose up to the flames, then that is truer than anything in the end. Custer identified as a person of the distant fires.

'I am wolf,' the cripple whispers. 'Not nothing.'

GAS STATION

Winter creaks into spring, like a door pushed open. Jamie takes a right at the fork in the road. One way leads into Harmswood, past the church, the school, and out through the trailer park to the water tower where the world ends. The other road gives way to dirt. He walks to the gas station, now closed down. Empty squares of glass plastered with stickers. Wind whistles through the place like when a person is missing teeth. It gives the building a voice, a human quality. Jamie takes a few steps over grass that bursts through openings in the concrete, tufts of green fire. Ivy hangs above him in nooses and swallows flutter in and out of mud nests. He watches a mother fly through a leafy loop and up to three crimson mouths, open like split figs. Worms get pulled apart from beak to beak.

A car groans behind him in the near distance. It draws closer at a steady pace. A beetle's shell beneath the sun. Funny how sound travels so clearly in emptiness, water dripping in a cave. Jamie spots it out of the corner of his eye. Moves in a little closer and remembers the dog. How he'd push the fur back and listen to see if its breath was any different from his own. Like all dogs, that one has gone now and Jamie is left looking at cracks in the concrete. He stares at the spot where two years prior Custer talked him out of ending his life. The gas station is deserted, everything vanished overnight as if a strong wind blew Custer up into the heavens like dandelion seeds. Carried him off to be planted elsewhere, in some other shit town, where a brand-new gas station would sprout through cracks in the asphalt. Swallows still build their mud-nests and feed death to their young. He'd done it all. Whatever was asked.

Jamie puts his backpack down. The ripped strap flaps open. It is a beautiful morning. The sun a perfect marble. He reaches into his pocket and takes out the last pouch of Custer's tobacco. Rolls it up tight. The empty store feels like it's laughing at him. Like the whole thing was a cruel prank. The door swings wide open in the breeze and slams shut. When he sparks the cigarette, the smell makes him think of moonflowers, opening up wide to the night sky. A different kind of breathing. He sits down and sends the smoke out in a neat jet which unfolds through a sunbeam. Smoke gives the soul a shape. An engine switches off like it had been running his whole life, like if it hadn't abruptly turned off, he'd never had known it existed. He turns to face a man, held together by a goatee and sunglasses. Jamie scratches his freshly shaved scalp.

'Hey, kid,' he says. The accent pangs. He forgets that there are other places. Blake is in one of those other towns. One of those other places, with other people.

'You know a Mary-Anne Bowery?' he continues.

Jamie shrugs and looks down. Sound builds in his ears, crickets chirping over a stagnant bog, movements beneath the surface.

'She's missing. I know you know that. Her father tells me you two'd been fooling around. He wasn't best pleased,' he says, looking just above Jamie's head.

'I know you, mister?' says Jamie. The man coughs into an open hand, shakes his head swallowing.

'Nope. But I know you. I'm looking into some disappearances throughout northwest of the state. You seen anything out of sorts?' His voice is bland. Jamie freezes but he won't let it show, he won't let his flames shimmer through the ice. Custer had warned him about what would come after he was gone. He must play dead again.

'I ain't seen her. We broke it off. Her Daddy wanted to put me in the hole. I'm a dropout,' says Jamie.

'They say you've been hanging with a real twisted crowd. Indian Nam vets and Peckerwoods from what I hear. You think any of them might know something about this poor girl?' He says pressing a foot into a green stem, smudging it over the concrete.

'Nope. Native folks always have a grudge against us anyhow,' says Jamie.

'Does anyone in this place know why they might have a grudge?' says the man, tightening.

'They're Injuns. They'll always hate us,' says Jamie, under his breath.

The detective stares down at the ground between him and Jamie. A large vein on the side of his head wriggles. Jamie fixes his eyes on a birthmark through the thinning hair.

'I'll be in town. Here's my card. If you know or hear anything from Miss Bowery, give me a call on that number,' he says handing out a white card with black digits. The faded head of an eagle. The car door slams shut. The engine starts up and he pulls out of the gas station. They are burning fields over the way in the next state, natives did this each year at the tail-end of winter. Crops finally purged.

Keep the fire buried. This is what Custer kept telling him at the end.

CUSTER

There was once a woman who, in transforming, gave herself up. She ran into the mountains and there was turned into a bird. It had to be this way. They had to have their bride. They demanded this and other things. Custer has closed the circle now. The snake has eaten its tail. With the boy, he has made it right and they would move into the afterlife together. It is time to leave. Time to follow Little Deer into the deep thicket. Time to let the past go and transform. Become one with the creek, the soil and the larvae of blowflies.

He tells Oklahoma and Missouri to unleash the dog ahead and wheel him up to the tree line. He will crawl from there on. Crawl until he can crawl no longer. He will give himself back willingly. He clips the brakes on each side of the wheelchair and the two men heave him up from under the armpits. Lay him down on his stomach gently as a babe. The boy understands his purpose, knows he's servicing something greater than himself. He's always known. They'd been there from the start, getting him ready, plucking him from the nest, showing him the colors in himself. Custer ignores the human side, the pleading weakness. The boy had given himself over willingly. This is right, this is just, this is the consequence of killing the gods' children. That is what Custer has always told himself in quiet moments. They don't ask. They just take.

His two companions will flee Harmswood—they know how to become ghosts. As he pulls on the earth with his hands once more, there is no reason to turn and look at them. It has all been said, all been done. It all comes back in the end as he pulls himself over the harsh ground deeper and deeper, following the distant shape of his sister, and a screech owl cries three times. She is alive in all the birds of existence.

One and the same female. The legless veteran pulls himself across the field. Back into the pinewood to find his buried heart. It will all burn down in the light of distant fires.

MOURNING FIELDS

This dream is old. People cry in it. Rope stretched out real thin to where it snaps and Jamie bolts upright in the whiplash-echo. Through the pines, church bells swell. 'Will Blake feel their mother's death?' he thinks. Will he hear those bells ringing through space-time? Maybe not. Vern'd been taking care of Ma. She'd been slipping and slipping through the years. The woods had grown thicker, curled around the house Jamie was born into, lifted up the floorboards, coiled around the plywood ready to drag it all under like a giant squid would a ship.

She slept a lot when they were young. Vern would push his way into a wall of black, bringing her soup and a little liquor. She slept like mountains. They'd hear them talk from behind closed doors. She'd be out in the night pacing. Jamie caught glimpses in his child's mind. Maw was beautiful in the moonlight, in her nightgown. Diaphanous, soiled at the fringe. There were stages before she was strong enough to take the men back in. The last was playing the same record over and over. Sickness, long sleep, walks in the dark. Blake slept through it all as Jamie watched.

Maw got evil in the last days. She thought the Howlers were hunting her. Prowling around the house, wood on the porch creaked under their feet, roof tiles slipped and cracked as they climbed over her. In the end, half her face sagged to the floor. She was being pulled down into the old mine shafts, like so many beautiful houses. Even Vern was scared of her. She couldn't get out of her chair, not even to walk to the washroom. Jamie hadn't seen her in weeks, months, maybe more. Maybe much more. Time had changed shape since he'd been sleeping out in the wild. It had grown in to a type of vine that blossomed and withered. He judged each day by what the birds did and how the trees sounded. He'd sometimes watch the house from the asphalt. Watch Vern going back and forth with shears and big rolls of wire. He'd stare at the shit-covered roof and feel a tightness in the chest. An event horizon for a porch light. Men killed the gods in deer season. Only the dogs knew he was there in the long grass watching. He is lying in his sleeping bag, in what used to be the mess hall of the school. The shadiest spot in summer. As the church-bells toll, he knows. He knows the rope has snapped and gathers his things. Wraps them up in a ball. He'll hitch a ride or walk the whole way. Whatever it takes. He has to see her in a box. To be there when they put her in the ground.

No one gives him a ride. Even those who are going that way pretend they don't see him walking. Jamie gives up and lowers his arm. He's made his bed and he'll lie in it. He wonders whether the men will show up for her. Whether they'll stay hiding and geld more animals to cut her out of them. In some ways, Maw helped keep the balance more than Vern ever did. She got Jamie out of the hole couple of times. Jamie knows his origin story is a tragic farce. That he's anyone's pup. A little way to walk yet. A little further. He passes the pay phone. Warped like a tree in the wind. Blake left a number and he called it many times. After he smoked a little too much and the world was getting to melt and waver. He wanted to hear his brother's voice. To hear the blood sing. Called and hung up. Walked all the way up only to walk back again. Behind the cage-bars of hallucination, all he wanted to do was sing. Custer is gone. Blown back down into the heart. The others had to run after it happened. Jamie chose to stay, chose to see things through once and for all. Mothers are supposed to protect their young. Maw and Vern were black holes, collapsed in the middle, letting no light escape beyond the brim of their eyes.

Pickups are parked out front. Vern won't be glad to see him.

Jamie turns and his feet hit the gravel. No crickets chirp this time. Maw's chair empty on the porch. The front door wide open for the mourners and the church-bells keep swinging out west bringing the tides in. Ja-mie is hit by a plume from the armpits. The smell of himself. Exposed like some kind of fiend. He throws down his bag, starts digging in for something cleaner, something less worn. He thinks of leaving, turning around, heading back to the school. But he can't, he can't run this time. Under his boots, a trail of ants goes about its business, in and out of the world beneath this one, appearing and disappearing—here and elsewhere. A large crow cackles on the telephone wire.

'Don't think you're coming in here. Not that way,' says Vern from the door.

'I come to see her. Same as everyone else,' he says. Vern stares silently. Jamie feels the people murmuring in the front room. Circling her body. He pictures grass growing up through her bones, flowers through her chest with bees buzzing, the wings of butterflies opening up like breath. A drip at the back of his throat. The sour taste of the cut. Vern walks up to him an arm up over his nose and mouth, brows furrowed. Even for him, Jamie is a shock, a wild man, a loon. He takes him in like a rare breed.

'You'll wash up in the back first, you hear?' he says in a hushed way.

'Yessir,' says Jamie.

'I'll dig up something for you to throw on. Go on, git. Don't let no one see you. There's soap back there. Make sure to use it,' he says.

'Yessir,' says Jamie and heads out back to the pump where they used to water the animals. Out back where the barrels are, the hydration pipes looped. He strips off all his rags without thinking. He steps over the line of ants. He pushes the lever down, once, twice, three times until it gargles like a throat. Shoves his head under the spout and lets the water wash over him, wash the forest away. He scrubs it out of every crevice, every crease in his body. Vern watches him wash. Walks over and drops lye soap on the ground like hard cheese. Jamie rubs himself raw. Rubs out the night.

Not many people have turned up. Only older folk peter in and out. The ones that remembered Maw as young girl. Who knew her as little Agatha. They shake Vern's hand through his veil of pipe smoke, he looks sicker than anything. Jamie stands in the doorway. A hand plays with the same stolen zippo he's had since childhood. Carved with some man's initials, something to leave behind, something to let someone know they were once around like a dinosaur bone. He flicks it open and back down again.

He sits down in the kitchen with his back to the room. The clothes itch badly. Sleeves come right up over his knuckles. He looks up at the stains on the ceiling like old friends. If you put your ear close enough to the walls, he reckons you could still hear moaning. Words caught between the plywood. Wallpaper is heaped in a pile like leaves. He thought about coming back for the five-string guitar, but it didn't feel right after Blake split. The wormhole at the center of Harmswood widened and pulled at each person. Jamie knew too much, way too much. He pulls out a smoke from some stranger's pack on the table. The grass rustles through the window like there's something digging. He flicks again and again but the chamber is all dried out. Slams it on the table threading his fingers behind his head. Vern comes and stands by his side staring out the same window. He leans over and bangs his pipe into the sink.

'Something's ripped the goats,' he says, more into the drain than to his nephew. 'Some bastard thing's gotten in again.' He flicks a yellow tongue over his dentures. Jamie remembers when he got those fitted, when the last tooth was wrenched out with pliers in the barn by a heavy-handed neighbor. Vern hates the goats, they remind him of being less, of his name drowning under a wave of turquoise.

'What if it's a person that's done it?' says Jamie. 'Wolves never leave a thing half eaten.' Vern bangs the pipe again. Makes a smacking sound with his lips.

'What the hell do you know about wolves?' he says quietly and walks back into the other room. People circle the box. The Horshams from two farms over pay their respects. A sparrow-like man, all loose skin and his wife try to make small talk with hands behind their backs, heads bowed. Talking next year's crop. How they could throw some work Vern's way. The place has gone to shit since Maw took ill. Dust all over, dishes congealing with pan grease. Judgement rains down. Some loggers poke their heads in. Roll up and shake Vern's hand, leaving it too long before they let go. Jamie feels a sharp pain watching it, this cruel tease. They're still blood in a way. None of the trappers show. All these men. Jamie tries to crawl through each moment, no matter how loudly the walls whisper.

Sue Batty arrived at daybreak. Clutching hand-picked wild flowers, a handkerchief pressed to her face. She waited loyal as a hound before Vern let her in. Jamie hasn't seen her in a good while. A lump forms in his throat for the library days. She looks down at his mother, glides her hand through the thin powdered hair. That cage of a head. He drags on the smoke and looks away to the grass. Blake bailed on them all, took off and never looked back. Part of him thinks he shouldn't be here either. There was someone he didn't know in that casket. Someone he'd never truly met. The thing outside has stopped digging.

By noon, all the mourners are gone. Vern collapsed in Ma's armchair, inspecting the dirt beneath his fingernails. The cuckoo clock ticks through the house, louder and louder. Jamie doesn't know what his uncle will do now. Now that he's lost this half of himself and it is almost deer season. The image of him barefoot, mascara running from his eyes, women's clothes tight over his body. What will he do now that the cord has been severed for good? Jamie sees those blackened feet dragging—the smell of bonfire and slaughterhouse.

Sue has her hands in her lap. A breeze glides in through the screen door. Jamie misses his brother in the deepest ways. The unspoken ways. Wishes he remembered more stories, more myths. About how the Vikings dealt with it. Wishes he could read better. Wishes he could forget better, that he didn't know so much about everything that happens in this shit town. When he turns, Vern is looking, a meat hook behind the eyes.

'Why're you here?' he says.

Jamie exhales. He's been in the mountains getting strong.

'She's my Ma. You got something say?' he says.

'You watch how you talk to me in this house. You watch how you speak, cos you owe me your soul, bastard, you hear?' He's drunk. 'Biggest mistake of my life was letting you live.' He gets up and falls back in the chair. Sue coughs behind her teeth.

'Letting me live? Only thing I owe you is a beating, you old bitch,' says Jamie and stands up. Vern's frown deepens like God's hand clenching into a fist.

'You think you know things?' he says. Jamie's wolves put their ears back. The past is still happening, still kicking its legs to be freed. That child is still in there. Sue looks up. Handkerchief in a ball, jowls quiver.

'God knows you're a liar. All bastards are. Born of a lie. I'll still knock you to the ground, boy. I ain't that far gone.' He stammers a little. Jamie's teeth grind against each other.

'I seen things. Out there where the sun don't shine,' he says.

'You have, huh? Well, I know you almost killed my sister when I pulled you from her belly,' he lifts his hands up, all veiny, grotesque. Large freckles from the sun. 'These hands. I'm the only reason you're breathing this air boy. Don't tell me about knowing and not knowing, cos you're just as soft as your brother. It's men like me, don't you forget it,' he yells the last few words. Puffs air into his skinny cheeks and takes a bottle from the cabinet, uncorks it, pours.

'I'm so sick of trying to do right,' he says after he downs the first.

'What you do at night, is that right?' says Jamie. Vern downs a second and a third. Back turned. Sue is cold as blue stone. A far away bleat makes her jump in her chair.

'She wanted me to leave you out there, you know. She wanted you gone. She wanted to forget you were ever inside her. She wanted to forget the garbage that squirted you into her. Do you know that?' Downs another.

'Calm down Vernon,' Sue mutters. 'This isn't the time. Not

today.' Vern shakes his head.

'You hid things, too, Mrs. Batty, and this is still my house,' he says. Sue looks back down at Ma. 'You know why we're different? We're pure. We understand the world. When others were scurrying down holes into the mines, our ancestors were up in the Teeth hunting devils. We know what needs to be done. Blood is all that matters, to them and to us,' he says and pours the rest of the liquor down him. 'Battys and Ackermans have kept company down the acres of time.' Jamie's hands shake. He loosens the shirt collar, his whole body under those clothes is being scrubbed by a steel brush. Where is the panther. The painter. The Whistling Wampus. To break in through the windows, grab him by the scruff of the neck and carry him off into the wilderness, back to the foot of the nothing-door. He strains to hear the big cat whistling in the tall grass, that siren. But nothing. Only Vern's hoarse rattle.

'This is enough liquor talk,' Sue says and pulls a stray hair from Ma's forehead. Vern shakes his head like a cow trying to get rid of an angry yellow-jacket.

'If not now, when?' he whispers, filling his pipe. Tobacco scatters. 'If not now, when? When will it end? It all comes back in the end that's all I know. It's all I've ever known. They don't ask, they just take.' His voice goes even higher.

'I think it's time you both left now. Let us be here,' he says, pulling his nose across the sleeve. 'Go on, before I slap you upside your face.' he says, and throws the pipe across the room. Presses both hands to his face. Sue is rigid, suddenly dry. She wraps her arm around Jamie, gently pulls him through the front room and out on the porch where Maw squinted at the world on a good day. They climb into her car and pull onto the asphalt. Jamie remembers the sound of his mother singing to the trees. A simple song, repeated again and again.

One's unlucky

Two's lucky

Three's health

Four's wealth

Five's sickness

Six's death.

Crows gather. All that sight, gone.

HECATE

Vern's curses curdle. Sue takes a sharp left past the library. She pulls up outside her small house. Graffiti scrawled over the door. Kids spray painted all manner of obscenities after her husband took his life. Ru-mors spread that they were both deep into devil-worship. That they sacrificed their own child. They called Sue a crone and a witch. She leans her head on the steering wheel, yelping like a beat seal. Jamie sits there as her back arches and falls. He twists in his seat and scrubs both hands over his scalp pushes the heels into burning eye sockets with weariness. Sue blows her nose like a foghorn. Takes off her glasses to dry the tears. Bats her face, embarrassed.

'Can we get out?' he asks.

'Where've you been son? You look half gone,' she says snuffling. 'Come in and I'll fix you a drink.' Jamie nods his head. So tired. Her hand is cupped in-between his shoulders as they walk up the path. Her house smells of damp and old cabbage. Jamie sees the couch and collapses. His heart is a monkey drumming. He hasn't smoked the cut in a real long time now and the air is sharpened, too bright. Sue shuffles around not knowing where to put herself.

'Ever had eggshell tea? Would you like that? Would you like an old Ozark trick to fix the soul?' she asks.

'Mhmm,' Jamie isn't listening. The arm of the couch reminds him of Sarah's dough arms, the pillowing flesh against his head feels so good. Jamie remembers the lights going out a lot at Aunt Sarah's. Hers was one of the best kept trailers. She'd managed to buy it flat out and took pride in keeping it nice, painted over the bleakness with warm colors. Deep red everywhere. She would take him into her vegetable patch and show him how the peppers grew, how orchids opened. Together they hooked eggs from nests and fried them up in butter. She saved animals and nursed them back to health however sickly they seemed. Once she went and took six baby bats from a neighbor's attic who was too scared to touch them. She plucked them from the ceiling like little flower buds and put them all in a shoebox but didn't see a slit in the side. Jamie had the box on his lap and as they drove along, one by one they slipped out and were flying around their heads. They both burst out laughing so hard she hammered the steering wheel, her face creased up and red like a newborn babe. She stopped just before the trailer park and opened up the windows so they all flew out into the darkness. They all found their home. Maw preferred candles and threw shawls over lamps to keep things dim. She never had much time for vegetables, just the slaughtered meat Vern brought back. Picking at a sheep's eyeballs with a toothpick.

He curls up in that memory. Crockery clinks in the kitchen. A kettle boils on the stove. Knowing Sue Batty is fixing him something feels good. So strange being indoors after all this time, so far away from the school. No one would come looking for him here. No one cared for white trash. The kettle squeals and Sue hums while pouring out the tea. Takes out a small bottle of brandy and adds drops into the fuming liquid. Shards of eggshell jiggle on the surface. Jamie watches the por-celain fragments dance under his heavy eyelids.

'Slowly now or you'll burn your tongue clean off,' she says.

'Thank you, Mrs. Batty. You know me and my uncle, we have problems. It's never been good,' he says and is surprised by how easily the words flow. Sue nods, sipping on her tea. His tongue burns like she said it would, his bottom lip grows fish-scales. The brandy helps soothe him, lull him in deeper.

'Agatha and I were real close as girls. Vern was always a little ghoul in the background. He followed us around. Creepy little guy. We caught him spying through windows when we bathed. When we danced by the papaw tree and I chased him off while she laughed and laughed. Don't tell anyone, but… sometimes your Maw liked to dress him up as a girl and call him Betsy. He was real good at playing the girl. Strange for such a big man, such an angry man.' She sips and swallows.

'Think I saw Betsy once,' he mumbles.

'I loved her so much, Jamie boy. She was always too good for this place. Your brother made a smart choice. A sharp choice,' she says.

'He sure did,' Jamie says as the brandy hits. 'He was always better than this.'

'Where've you been son?' she says again reaching for his hand. 'What's taken you? I see it moving in there, looking right back at me.' A pinecone clatters onto the porch. 'You know there are all sorts roam-ing around this season. They say wolves are coming back. Can't remem-ber last time I seen a wolf,' she says and lifts the mug to her lips.

'They're better off hidden,' says Jamie. There are no photo-graphs in Sue's place, no mirrors, no Jesus strung up. He sits up a lit-tle straighter. Wipes his eyes. The unwashed fabric bites. Vern must've pulled it from the depths of hell. Jamie looks at Sue squarely as a wind blows pulling things out of the trees, making the soul sneeze. 'I just prefer it out there, less is more. Don't they say that?'

'They say a lot of things, Jamie Ackerman,' she says, pulling locked onto her a loose thread from her cardigan, looping it around her finger until it bursts with maroon. 'But the things that live in there take no prisoners. They've been out there and we've been down here. You are born into a state of affairs and it becomes normal.' Her eyes stay blood-puffed thumb. Another pinecone thuds the wood.

'I've been out there since I could stand on these legs. I've al-ways known and I'm on their side,' he says, searching his pockets for a cigarette. Smoking was a knot tied to Blake, tied tightly to his voice somehow and the things he'd say to tame Jamie's mind. But right now, all he can think about is lighting up, anything. He finds a dead moth, its wings crumble to dust in his palm.

'Any spare smokes laying around?' he says, restless and exhaust-ed. Sue stands up a little too quickly. Blue and white spots spread out in front of her from a rush of blood to the brain. 'Carl had some cartons. They may have rotted by now. You're welcome to them.' She shuffles off to the back of the house. It is dim at Sue Batty's place. The drapes are drawn, faded from absorbing sunlight. He's forgotten the feel of houses, of furniture, roofs that don't drip or howl in the wind. She throws him three packs. A dead man's packs. They all have the softness of paper about to melt.

'I'd ask you to step outside. But you go ahead and light up. Seeing as the day is what it is,' she says. Jamie nods, takes a bitter drag and kills it in a glass of water. There really is nothing else other than the cut from now on. Sue shifts her buttocks and clears her throat. The air glows and quivers between them.

'Agatha spoke to me once about our boy. Poor thing. This is no place for a child like that,' she says, building. Up and up, gathering. A scratching behind the door. Wanting to come out, feels claws on the wood, drool hanging.

'Your Maw was hard. I'm not saying she was right. Things she did I can't find room in my heart to forgive. Her Daddy never let go of her even in death,' she says.

'I know why I did what I did. I know why I didn't want my brother to see what I saw. No one needs to live with that in their head,' says Jamie. Pins and needles. Sue fades, she bleeds back into the walls and is sucked down through the rug and the floorboards into the base-ment below. The tea and brandy evaporate and he shrinks down into the child he's been hiding. He falls back, through his skull, straps him-self into the past, chained. Sue's marshmallow voice pulls him back in from that day that spins inside like a wheel.

'I can't remember him alive. An easy target for perverts I guess, all slow like that,' mutters Jamie. He scratches and itch on his arm that isn't there. Crawling over his skin.

'You know, it's not just elk we hunt in deer season,' she says, half-smiling.

'Wilf Batty was a bastard. That's why it's hard to shake. It could've been me, or Blake—who'll miss a bastard? We're never sup-posed to be here anyhow. He was left on your doorstep wrapped in dirty blanket. They said it was a miracle,' he says. Sue sighs.

'He was one of your Ma's. She gave him to us. One of the many that never were. Vern pulled him from her like he did you, like he did Blake and all the rest. Most of them stillborns. She only kept the two of you. The rest he took out there, left by the trees.' Breathe. Where are the wolves? Where is the panther?

'She wanted you gone too, after she saw those legs. But Vern couldn't do it. He brought you back,' her voice trails off like the tail of a falling star. Collapses into space.

Jamie listens. But something in his head switches off, retreats into a shell. The couch cushions soft against his face. The words she speaks are the bones of so many children piled up to the ceiling. They pour into the small house. Burst through the windows like an ava-lanche, cascading over the furniture, over both of them. Small bones, bigger bones—femurs, ribs, pelvis all collide and clatter in a xylophone hymn.

'I'll lay my head down,' he says as the bones smother him, the laughing skulls.

Sue throws a blanket over him, right up to the neck. His face is gray, cheeks pulled in, raw rashes all over. She feels how she used to feel turning all the lights out in the library, leaving the lost boy under a stack of chairs. She makes sure the drapes are drawn tight. Agatha's boy can stay as long as he wants. If the moon is right.

OUT ON PLUTO

No river in his ears, no wind, no critters snuffling. He has slept. Deep-ly. From morning through to the early hours of the next morning and then some. A tree's sleep. The darkness has lost its velvet, it doesn't sing back. Without Custer's cut burning, the world smoothens out into a field. Jamie pushes himself up, moonlight slides between the drapes. A crunch around the rim of each thought. An eggshell feeling.

Maw in the box. She looked like a fish hidden under the same rock for a hundred years. Untouched by the light. Jamie knows that many drank to her memory. From behind closed doors. After they cursed out their families and fed the animals. They looked out into the distance with nothing but a limp cigarette for company. They'd miss her, they'd miss that part of themselves. Jamie exhales into the sour black room. He slept through the funeral. Eggshells keep crunching inside him. The tea sits heavy. He tries to stay as still so as not to stir the brain and topple the pyramid of little skeletons. Pinecones roll down the rafters. A storm must be gathering. Jamie leans forward and picks up the cigarette pack. It felt so bad earlier, sickly in his chest. Hooks of smoke. A branch cracks. An animal squeals. Sue's words poke through the mass of bones. Still there, waiting, the truth has gone nowhere. Their loggerhead brother, butchered, dressed out and drained hanging like an offering. Maw's porcelain profile, her scraggly wisps of hair lifting as the door opened and the fields yawned.

Jamie tries to cough. Again and again, but can't. A rope creaks. Wilf is in the room. They are all there. The lost. The air still won't crawl out of him. His skull is fingers tapping the glass. Thick and leathery, strong fingers that have no mercy and no patience—

voice, that vibrating cello just hunger. He coughs again slamming a fist into his chest, something dislodges, he lets it out and the walls shiver. Jamie hopes he hasn't woken Sue. He couldn't bear to hear another note of her string.

He has to run. Custer knew best. Jamie is good in the dark, when there is nothing but a blurry wall of eyelid. His boots are by the door and there is nothing else to take. The wolves will never return. There is an absence where there was once paws padding. He bends to tie the muddy laces. Keeps messing up and having to re-tie over and over. Nothing compares to the pain of truth, nothing in the world compares to knowing. Batty's body keeps swinging somewhere in the black of Sue's living room as he forgets how to tie laces, forgets how to use his fingers, back and forth in the fall, inside the blue body of smoke.

Jamie feels it coming. Fire eating everything. Not even a stick through the eyeball can stop it. He throws the boots off and feels for the door handle, frees himself. Lifts the latch up and the twilight licks his face. He leaves Wilf Batty swinging. Barefoot he walks out into the night. He can smell Vern all over him. Something big runs into the grass under a streetlight. Jamie pretends not to see it. Behind the house there is a noise, a murmuring. The moon half there. Keeping an eye on everything beneath her toes. Stones, twigs and mouse skeletons claw into his bare soles. He passes a tree, with a broken limb that came off in the wind. The murmur hangs, each string of an instrument cut off with garden shears. A human voice. The worst of a human voice. Tears sting the corners of his eyes. The tops of his cheeks seethe like water in a hot pan. Fear. He is afraid. More nothing than wolf.

He crouches and peeks from behind an incinerator. Out in

the backyard, Sue is naked. Singing into the darkness, her hands crescent moons and sea anemones. He watches her, the body seen and unseen as the light rises and the birds start chirping. Pillowy folds in the half light, her eyelids flutter, her eyes roll up. Breath drags on the ribcage. The quiver of jowl as she gurgles and whines. Crescent moons and sea anemones. She warbles to the thin black line of trees across the field. She is an underwater mammal; the twilight makes her so. Her spine, curved like a tusk. Maw's gone nowhere. She is in that dance, in that calling. Ready to mate with the wild.

There are more of them behind her. Naked bodies. Over the smoky ground they lie. Rolling and tossing. Hands and mouths grasp-ing at the loose flesh. Breasts and buttocks, genitalia and armpits. Wres-tling beneath the fingers of the moon, under the little deaths of stars and wormholes—this is what happened at night, this was the split, the underworld. This was a backwoods middle finger. Creation-critters fornicating. This orgy in a town of a thousand people. The old timers. This was their ritual. This is where they came from. All of these ways, that made no sense anywhere else but here. It seemed part of the natu-ral order. The knowledge of it runs deep, passed down through blood and breath. A memory slipped in at birth. They are trying to get the crop high.

The rye and the barley started going black with parasites. They said when the moon was on the right side, a man and a woman would have to do it in a field and make sure they sowed the seed for a healthy crop. Jamie watches as some of them get up and run naked up and down the length of the field three times. The space inside his bones opens up and screams. He runs. Bare feet scrape the rough ground. Pain is nothing at the end of the world. He takes off left, running down the asphalt and into town. Streetlights flicker. All is a ritual. The farm-ers will be getting up, milking udders fit to burst. The soft patter of his feet, the funny flail of his legs. The reason for all of it can be summed up in those crooked limbs. A tire swings tied to a branch as he rushes past. Something runs beside him in the tall grass. He pretends it isn't as big as all the Ozarks combined, large as the hole left by Blake.

He runs past Mary Anne's. God only knows where she is now. He wishes he knew and yet is grateful for not knowing. Spared one jagged truth. He hopes she just split like his brother. A light comes on. He runs all the way to Burnt Mill and there finds the open plot where they lay Maw to rest. Finds it empty. An empty urn. The womb, the cave, the hole in the ground. They didn't bury her with her eyes facing down. Jamie jumps down inside it and lays there, hugging his sides.

He pretends to catch fire.

TITANOMACHIA

In exile people become beasts. It is hard to explain to those who haven't lived it. Jamie sometimes wonders about how that might feel, meeting someone that has no idea, who doesn't believe hell exists. A boredom that breaks the mind. *Here be dragons*, he would tell that person. This patch of land they used to mark with lions and sea creatures. A bored man is a man who isn't a man. Everyone out here has been left to die of exposure. No, he'd say nothing. If you grow up poor, you say nothing and let the rain piss down.

The clouds are knitted brows as a storm steps in closer. Jamie runs a hand over his scalp. Thinks of when Bull was in the picture. Back when they smashed and spray painted their way into the world, making space for themselves. The rain is devils hopping from stone to the next. Jamie stares up into the sky from the oblong hole, up from his mother's womb. They burned her up in the end, a change of heart.

A car pulls up. Men approach. He can always tell. Part of him feels stupid. Weak for crawling back into her only to find that she was never there. The gate clangs open. He has lived through this before. Always hit first. Go for the throat and balls. He stays down there in the fetal position, soaked. Some pair of eyes saw him running through the night, called it in, licked their lips, clicked the joints in their fingers. This will be a sloppy beating. Thought and memory fly away towards the Teeth.

Three red faces peer down. Day drinkers. Mary-Anne's father and two others beside him. Unsteady above the knees. A huge flock of starlings swirls over their heads. The storm is still gathering, rolling in from beyond the borders of the map. Mary-Anne's father swallows, stubble has grown over his features. Hard to see his eyeballs beneath the baseball cap.

'What you looking for down there, Ackerman? Your Maw?' he says quietly.

Wolves. Wolves are behind everything. Wolves have been there since the beginning, they move behind the sun and the moon, inside the rhythm of everything. When the whole world was still an egg with a snake coiled around it, wolves were there sniffing, testing always test-ing.

'Didn't tell you they burnt her up, huh? That bat-shit uncle of yours has a sense of humor. I'll give him that,' he says.

Cowards travel in threes. Jamie makes his stomach a stone. Bowery spits like a teenager playing tough. Jamie climbs out of the hole meant for his mother and stands up straight. Gaunt and sleepless. Haunted by Sue moving alone, naked in the darkness. By the sound coming out of her like she was expecting an answer. One of the others steps forward, fat and bearded, oil stains down his shirt. He puts on what he thinks is a hard voice.

'Mamma Ackerman pushed out so many turds, Harmswood owes her half its folk,' he says. Jamie looks at him, observes the beady eyes and bad skin, the drinker's broken blood vessels.

'I remember you,' Jamie says pointing. 'I remember her laugh-ing about you. How you were itty bitty, a little shroom. She couldn't even feel it,' he says opening up a small space between his thumb and index. 'Itty bitty small,' he says and smiles.

Always so easy to get under their skin. He had dirt on every-one. All the ins and outs. Maw was needed. In Harmswood, the things people truly wanted were unseen. What Jamie wants now is to see the whole place set alight and burning. So, for once, everyone could live in clear sight of what occurs. Maw will slither around their minds, she'll whisper through the crackle of a cigarette. The father folds his arms. 'Where's my little girl?' he says through tremors. 'I know you know, just tell me no one's touched her. Tell me she's whole,' he says wide-eyed. Everyone remembers Wilf Batty. How he almost looked like an angel with his arms and legs folded back. Bowery's mouth hangs open.

'Don't know. Haven't seen her,' says Jamie.

'You made a whore out of my girl,' says Bowery.

'I hope she's gone. She'll make you proud in ways you'll never understand,' says Jamie. Bowery pauses, looking at the cripple. The bastard from beyond the trailer park.

'I seen you spray painting that Satanic shit,' he says to the others who nod. 'I can take you in for that. I can make hell real for you, boy.' A dirt bike screams in the distance and shroom-dick lunges, throws him down. Punched in the shell of his ear, thoughts white with pain. A boot to the tailbone. Two of them sit on his legs. They pull his arms back and push his face into the wet earth. 'Man is wolf to man,' Custer's voice in the shape of those starlings.

'I'll end you,' says Bowery and cuffs Jamie's wrists. He is one with the rain, inside each drop as it falls. The wolves whimper but he is smiling now. The murmuration scrawls the word, *Viking*, over a mangy slobbering mutt with three heads.

UNTIL THE SUN IS SWALLOWED BY A WOLF

Pluto is the same size as its closest moon. The human heart is the same size as a fist. Jamie tries to open up his eyes. He is lying on his back. No night birds, no gurgling, no caterpillar-nest heavens. This is a deeper space. Before splits opened in the sides of a creature, before legs sprout-ed. Before the wind seeped in and merged into one cold muscle. Jamie sings. To himself, to space. It all rings.

He can't move. A tight ball in his lungs. A pouch full of pins. Oceans rise in his cauliflower ear. People never stop thinking about the divinities they hold inside them, when there is nothing else. Jamie knows this is the end. He knows where he is. He has been here before. Anything they can pin on him, they will. His face is bloated and eyes puffed out like bee stings, nose cracked at the bridge. They beat his chicken legs with sticks. The hole smells of someone else and the moon slips in through a split in the concrete. Jamies coughs. Rain is always a comfort. Behind his eyelids, red snow is falling.

Mary-Anne's been missing a fortnight. She's never coming back and now they need someone to blame. The place gets nervous if there's no one to hang. Her pretty, dog-scarred face was plastered over the state. She was on the news. That same photograph. The awkward shape of her smile, like it was her duty to be lost. He has forgotten the sound of her voice. The toothpaste smell of her kisses. In the end, the heavy ancient thing that hid in the tall grass took him away from her em-brace. The last thing he'd done is give her some of Custer's cut by the water tower, and then nothing. Only waking up, cold and soiled like he used to. Her face was now nailed to the wood of every pylon along the asphalt, in town, staring back.

The smell of Blake never left. He could take Maw over the smell of that love any time. Maw and her empty grave, her body ashes. The spectacle of Sue alone, dancing into the night with her flesh exposed. He could take it all and swallow it, but the soft smell of biscuits and book pages left in a room by his brother was a real killer. It's why Custer's hands over his made a difference. Why his presence invited him into a kind of truth. Dazed and with his mind bucking like an unbroken horse, Jamie tries to speak. Croaks, boiling nails in the lar-ynx. He hoists himself upright against the wall. Coughs so the guards might hear.

When the gas station closed, a witch hunt began. Mobs of farmers, packs of them in pickups scoured the land with bats and shot-guns. Satanic Panic said a voice in the TV. An epidemic of baby-eating devil-worshippers was festering in every backwoods town in Ameri-ca. Cops beat the grass with billy sticks for Mary-Anne's body, blood-hound muzzles pulled in her scent from clothes and belongings. Funny how outsiders never heard the howls. Never noticed the yelps from the mountain. If they couldn't pin it on the Indians, it would have to be the next best thing. They needed someone new to burn.

Jamie hangs his head and spits between his feet. Everything hurts. That was some beating. Hasn't felt one of those since he caught Vern back in the day, when it was still happening with his brother. When Jamie broke through the trees screaming at the top of his lungs, growling like an animal and found his uncle bent over half dressed. Blake on his back, eyes fluttering to the sky. No, nothing compares to the beating he got on that day. Nothing compares to the fear of that beating. Nothing but the fear Bowery has for his daughter. If she was up in the Teeth, they'd never find her.

Blake's voice glides in and merges with Custer's. The color red keeps glowing behind his skull. The problem with childhood is that most of it is lost to a kind of twilight and no one ever truly knows. No one can possibly know what happened in the end. Jamie swallows hard as his skin opens up, every pore a little swallow's mouth. In the silence of the hole, Custer's voice wins out. A pain in his tailbone throbs. Bal-looning out into his lungs. Hours have passed, no food or water. His head is broken beer bottles. He tries to move his fingers. Puts a hand to his face and feels the texture of dried blood, up into his nostrils and over the lips, crusting. His clothes have been stripped off and he feels small. Laid bare. Reborn, as red eats into the turquoise.

Officers hum outside like fish wives. His ears ring so loudly he can't make out words, no caught fragments of language. Footsteps up and down the hall. It hasn't even begun. The sky is out of reach. The creek. The panther. He is out of reach. He feels night's smile deepening and someone unlocks the door. He tries to push up onto his elbows and the turquoise swells against bone and muscle. Each movement carved out of thin air.

They move over him. Pick him up and drag him into the tube of fluorescent light. His knees give way. They drag him like a sack of grain past everyone, the mess of him exposed. Chuckling. Gasps. He can barely see through those beaten eyes. Thrown into a chair and the door slams shut. Someone gives him a pair of shorts and he maneuvers into them, each leg a twisted root. Just opposite sits the charcoal out-line of a person. Jamie was naked then, too. When branches creaked and crashed. Sparks from matches fluttered all around him. Maw never wanted him. There were few things she did want, to never sleep again and to sleep forever. To forget about her children. That was one of the secrets. Blake pulled books in closer to his face until it was over. The sound of a cracked match is the world's hatching.

An ashtray is pushed across the table. The ringing in his head widens. Somewhere the fire is buried, but he can't feel it now. He is stripped bare beneath the vibrations of fluorescent lights. The charcoal man taps a pen on the desk. Jamie tries to open his swollen eyes a little wider. Crushes a plastic cup of water into his face, trying to drink. It is the detective that found him at Custer's. Sweat stains his shirt under the armpits. Jamie remembers his pin-sized head on a bull-thick neck. He remembers the faded head of an eagle.

'Hello again. We found some questionable items in your possession,' he says. 'Not exactly a devout Christian, are we? Sleeping in your dead mother's grave won't get you sympathy votes here kid. It'll be a lot easier for you if you give me something. The Bowery girl.' He taps the pen one final time. Clicks a red button on a black tape recorder. Wheels turn under the glass. A camera behind him blinks. Jamie starts to sway like after the accident. When he didn't speak for six days.

'You're not getting out of here unscathed,' he says and his words grow scales. Jamie looks up at him, his beat face slipping off the bone like chicken in soup. Pain squeezes him into the margins. The child inside him can't breathe.

'Smoke,' he says through teeth.

It isn't fear anymore. Never really was. Just a submission to violence. A crimson brushstroke through no-man's land. He pushes into the pain. Pushes in to escape and to merge. All of it has led him here—chained up waiting for oblivion. The detective knocks out two cigarettes, he lights them both in his mouth with a match and reaches over. Jamie thinks of using his jaws to tear and bite into the cheeks, going for the windpipe like a big cat. The cigarette dangles, trembling on his lip.

'Take me back, Jamie. How did you fall in so deep?' says the cop. 'I know you've been pushing dope for the Griffins. I don't care about that right now. Where's the old chief at?' His cigarette sits lodged in the ashtray. Jamie barely hears him, his head kills. Blood drips down the back of his throat like an answer to the tapping pen.

'Look, I don't think you're bad. Just a little lost,' he says.

'I'm not lost,' says Jamie under his breath. The sound of a car speeding off on the other side of the interrogation room.

'They brought me in because this goes beyond you. It's bigger than your screw-ups. I know all of it and it's garbage. In every shit town, there's a kid like you that feels different, I get that. What I want to know is why people here hate your family. Why will no one will talk to me about you guys?' A drug-dog barks at nothing in the hall.

'You won't find her,' says Jamie. 'She's their bride now.' A coldness, a breath from the outside. The detective stiffens and Jamie draws in a drag, right up to the filter. 'You won't get far here mister. You might wanna turn tail while you still can. Leave us to our own. We're another species down here,' he says and swallows loudly. The detective drops the pen.

'Whose bride, Ackerman?' he says.

Silence. Jamie tilts his head back.

'They want the death penalty. I'm all you've got here,' he says, pointing a finger into his chest. Jamie's thoughts melt. There's only so much to hold back, before the nest bursts. 'If you confess, I can buy you some time. I can get you life with parole.' He had seen his uncle carry bundles to the forest. For years, he thought it was just a dream. She'd fatten up, bloat like a heifer. There'd be a day and night of closed doors and sounds of slaughterhouse. Blood-ball screams. Then he would hear Vern's feet crunch over the ground. Cracking the air like glass. Jamie climbed out to see him walking. All the children she bore to a broken condom, left out like dogs and soup bones. The pinewood claimed all the world's unwanted parts.

Howls after he returned. Over the next nights, Jamie watched her fall to her knees, clutching at her nightgown, tearing at it. Burying her face in the wet grass as her twin dragged her back into the house. Blake had his back turned, facing the wall. Headphones keeping his skull in place, softly breathing with a book under his pillow. Jamie heard her scream ricochet back at whatever screamed in the first place. No, Maw hadn't wanted Jamie. He was born of that fat devil in her dreams. It was Vern who pulled him out; it was Vern who took him and brought him back. Some kindness. Some mercy. Or just too much whiskey, in a place God went to die.

The detective stares at his bloated face, he can feel his eyes searching.

'What about your brother?'

'Huh?'

'You talk to him?'

'No.'

'Fallen out?'

'No.'

'Then what?'

'He moved away,' says Jamie. 'He forgot about this place and that's how it should be. I'm glad. We're the living dead here.'

'Didn't you both discover a murdered child?'

'We did. Well, I did.'

'In the woods?'

'That's right.'

'Must have been hard seeing a thing like that,' he says. 'I've never seen a thing like that,' he says. 'Why did you blind him on that day Jamie? Why do that?'

'Like you said, it's hard seeing a thing like that. I reckoned one pair of eyes was enough,' he says.

'What else goes on under those pines, Jamie?' he says, pressing.

Jamie rocks back and forth. In a flurry, he pukes up blood onto the table, into the ashtray. Some splatters over the detective's cufflinks.

'Jesus,' he says, jumping back out of his seat. Shouts down the hall. Runs out to fetch towels. The dog hasn't stopped barking. It yanks on its chain head jolting back, a coil of resonance. Jamie catches a glimpse of Bowery in the corridor, eyes wide. He cradles a bound-up hand. Jamie tilts his head back and looks through his swelling flesh straight into the buzzing light of the ceiling.

On the last day, Custer covered his body in powdered bone. Goat, cow, coyote, turkey-vulture, screech-owl. Blended him in with the lost children of the residential school. Jamie is *thought* and unlike memory he has the clarity it takes to see things for what they are sometimes. That knowledge is fire. He knows now, at least he knows. The black drink tasted of coffee beans and dirt. Custer pushed a handful of black rye fungus in after it. They were in the ruins where everything had happened all those years ago, that was still happening. When Custer opened his mouth afterwards, snakes fell from it coiling. The walls melted and people sobbed in the cave of his ear. Jamie understood then. All of his life has been fragments moving closer and closer together. Closer to black mountain peaks under a red sky. The only sound was the trickle of the creek whispering, coaxing. Something drew closer. Branches crashed, pinecones tumbled to the ground. Shrieks like laugher. Volcanic hunger in the pupil.

The gods are here,

       the gods are here,

              the gods are us.

Officers run in to mop up his blood. A red light from the video camera winks. The light expands and grows until it is growing through Jamie and out. Yells, curses, screams all too far away now. The room is thrumming. Beyond the singing rim. Through and way. The pain goes, eaten. He is through the nothing-door. Through to black ice and red snow. Flaming curtains shut on the world. The smell of sulphur and animal fat burning.

Part III.

White Noise to Birdsong.

CATHARTES-AURA

There is an animal called the hyena. It lives in the graves of dead men. Feeds on their bodies. By nature it is sometimes masculine, sometimes feminine—for that reason it is unclean. It follows sheepfolds. Creeps around men's houses. It makes a sound like a man being sick to lure out dogs so it can devour them. If hounds come into its shadow, they lose their voice.

BLAKE

Ditch-witches we called them back home. Women who lost themselves. Women who got up out of a deckchair, stripped their clothes off and walked bare into the night. They turned into cats or bats or owls. Though, like most things back home, they didn't really exist. I was surprised when I saw one in the city. I never knew her name. Only the rattle of her trolley, her possessions heaped high in a tower. Plastic bags hanging from either side. Many cats scratched the bags open, she talked to them like children. She dragged her whole world behind her with one hand, adding things. Her hair slowly meshing into a fat yellow dreadlock.

    I saw her on the subway and part of me chose to step into the same carriage. So we could be close. So I could listen to her garbled sentences through my headphones. Beer spurted from a can she pumped against her chest like a war drum. When a baby caught her eye, it broke my heart to see her soften. She said she had a son. She couldn't remember where she'd left him. She had a son somewhere and he was a good boy, a beautiful boy made of turtle doves and silk. Then she'd forget him and cackle. She'd chant in stomping garbage blues—I love you Mama— thumping her chest, stamping on commuters toes. I wanted to be the son she'd left behind. I wanted her to transform. Ever since I'd moved to the city, the ditch-witch had been there. Another human caught in life's teeth. She was wilderness in a sea of concrete. I wanted her to transform.

The first few years in the city were hard. I tried things in those first weeks I wish I hadn't. Made friends with back stabbers. I did everything to forget about home and it was all so loud inside me, all so alive and swarming outwards. Everything had a face, like childhood, but worse. A grinning, sneering mouth coming at me from mirrors, windows, in the eyes of people passing by. I wept every night in the beginning. When the booze membrane dissolved, all that was left was the hole I'd been tip-toeing around. The Bald-Knob was always in the room with me. But he could only eat what was already dead. Over time he had difficultly with memories that were still kicking and screaming—couldn't digest those, couldn't break them down. The poor creature landed and took off again clumsily, didn't know what to do with himself waddling around in my apartment like an old man dragging his limp wing.

I secured work as an English teacher after a string of jobs that were as lifeless as they were sustaining. I kept reading in my free time. Blabbed my way through the interview and was given a chance to blab some more. Blab on about the synthetic qualities of Whitman and cultish mythologizing of Yeats. I tried to show how poets puffed themselves up to youths of the inner city. I thought it might be interesting. The head mistress had one of those voices that crushed flowers into a notebook. I supplemented mostly. Called into action from the break room, a thick syllabus thrust into my hands. Stick to the book. I could tell all the teachers were former smokers, hiding behind a history of phlegm and stale breath. They chugged bottles of green juice to mask the cracked inside-of-a-pipe feel. I could tell that every one of them had a pack of cigarettes taped to the back of their toilet tank—little secrets kept to keep the blood warm.

The kids were rough around the edges but a dead eye gave me some clout, a kind of villainous mystique. We weren't too far apart agewise. I sneaked cigarettes with them during recess under a big fir tree. The boys wore their hoods up, all round shoulders, nodding heads, infected pores. The girls seemed more at ease with getting caught somehow. I killed my Arkansas twang before it got in the way, but the kids didn't even care. I told them a couple of stories from the mountains. The crazier ones that made no sense but satisfied a kind of childish perversion. They liked the one about a girl who got an eel stuck in her vagina. The hill-folk were aliens.

'Everything good comes from behind those words,' I would say while lingering on a stanza. 'Where everything collides and there are no lines, or borders, or cages separating us. Where our brains merge,' I said wanting to give them some of that light to keep close against the wide night. That road that wound out beyond adolescence like a soft tongue. Months went by. A year and then the next. The syllabus eaten up by dust and mold. 'We consider our staff family here,' said the head mistress before she fired me.

Something ached when I left those kids. Something strange and familiar all at once. The feeling reeked of wet leaves. My second job was at a small commercial art gallery. I don't know how; I don't know why. But this is where I started writing it all down. Through the dead shifts, in a forgotten corner of the city. I began to pull at the wet soil with badger claws, letting it spill out from under. I scribbled it down in notebooks, all jumbled and confusing. Through the tedious months of selling smug postcards, overpriced necklaces, and useless pottery. Months I enjoyed for what the words on the page gave me. The Bald-Knob hissed in my ear like the end of a record playing.

The language galloped in front of my thoughts. It was bastardized into a strange chorus of genres. A chaotic euphony crammed into the absence of a voice. All the fragments of prose I'd ever read. Facts, fiction, articles, manuals; they played and mated with each other behind my eyes and whispered to me through his crooked beak. It burned with truth, like holding a mirror up to the sun. I had the Bald-Knob inside my pen now. He wrote it for me. Wrote up the fragmented myth of my childhood. The door that kept something out. I couldn't let it open. I couldn't let whatever lived inside that chamber clamber out into the room with me. I wasn't like Vern but I was a mess. All the words were a different kind of animal, a creature that had a life of its own. Born out of me. I knew I would never show these to anyone. These private bestiaries.

Alcohol was a problem. A snake I couldn't behead. For a good while it swallowed me. Mornings were hangovers. They helped me focus on work like a well-trained monk painting penises with wings in the margins to fight through boredom. I didn't care as long as there was silence. The Bald-Knob bobbed his head up and down, animated. The snake laughed its guts out until someone noticed me suffering, noticed my hands quiver as I handed back loose change. A kind soul, a gallery intern noticed me squirming in my own skin. She gave me a number to call, an address to go to. I wouldn't have met Blue if it weren't for that gallery. I wouldn't have met the girl with the heavy-set jaw that cut me from the snake's belly like an antelope.

EMILY AND BLUE

Otherness is a thing from ghostly places. Since infancy she had felt other. This feeling blurred the lines between her, her skin, and the world at large. It made the world cruel, cold, like a cave of ice. No spirit animals lived in it, only the echoing thud of layers melting. Heaven melting above her. She gave birth to her own beasts, painfully funneled them into being and made that ice-cave their nest. To be other is to fall. Is to fail. Her mother left her to a home of drunk aunts, squealing baboon children, and men that came and went. Men that made everyone to chain-smoke in their wake. It made her look for small rooms in all of these places. Rooms that locked on the inside, where she could count down backwards from ten and push the impossible out with her tongue.

She had Polish blood. Her father looked like her. Deep lines on the sides of the nose. A thin membrane over every word. They looked most alike when he bit his lip, squinted his eyes. When Szymon stopped drinking, every light was too bright for him. He didn't know if his daughter was safe for consumption. He saw that there was something else looking back from beneath the child's blonde fringe. Something of himself that couldn't be faced without the substantial measures of liquor. He tugged a sleeve down, pushed her little hand away when she reached out to trace the inked digits on his forearm as if she were peeling a fresh scab.

Szymon was found dead on her fifth winter. Face down. In piss-stained American snow. The cold preserved him. The sun thawed him out and his powdery remains were handed over to his daughter in a lumpy plastic bag, which almost got mistaken for a hoover sack and thrown out with the house's trash. When she was old enough, she released him into the air. In the middle of the night, she shook him out wildly in spirals as the street cats watched. She hoped he'd be carried over the cities and forests of other landlocked states. Out to sea where the gulls and sea-lions could have him all to themselves. She kept nothing of Szymon. Nothing but thin membranes and deep lines.

Blue was once called Emily. Emily wasn't happy. Emily felt like a fetus, sprung from the womb too early. The name didn't match the person. It didn't fit her contours and edges, tight around the windpipe. The name Emily began to choke her, for it assumed things. Things that were meant for others, like drawings in children's books, stories that had no reason to include her. The person buried beneath this name got lost for a time. First, she read. Then, she wrote. Wrote it all down, as Emily: the unborn. These words climbed the walls. They were shotgun fire. The cruel world beyond her skin began to shatter and retreat, wounded. She stuck it right in the nether regions, right in its icy blue balls. Treading lightly through graffitied tunnels and alleyways in the hope that heaven had an outline she could cut out with scissors and roar through that slit in the cosmos. She wrote and when she spoke, it caught a heat. Like a tire spinning ferociously on a wet street. Her words were raw. Rid of membranes. They carried her out of the broken homes and halfway houses, gave a her a stage to stand on when the world was a trapdoor. Many shaking hands. Many nodding heads of approval. Heads and hands of people she should've known, should've thanked, whose feet she should have wanted to kiss and lick. That fuel, that shotgun pellet, was what those people called her work, her art, her poetry.

Emily numbed herself beyond the stage. The love she sought out in others was other in itself. It made the possibility of that love uncanny, ghostly. There were girls and women who came up to her after a reading. They held their hearts out in their hands, still beating. They asked her for more of what she couldn't give. To be shot over and over again. They offered her a smoke, then a rough lay and then lines in the restroom. Nevermore, evermore—the love was rolled up tightly and made her face opaque. All these girls with their hearts in their hands, almost tore her apart like the furies did Orpheus. They almost took her head and sent her lyre, unstrung, collapsed like a rib cage down the river. It was as if all the world's children had forced themselves into her little locked room. One of these furies got inside her head, ate her alive and left her for dead. A break-up. She hadn't been warned about the perils of letting someone else in. Someone that was somehow always the wrong someone. Without her words, her voice, the stage she so easily owned, that someone would never even have glanced in her direction. Orpheus was only as good as the notes quivering in his throat. After an award ceremony, after a book singing in the corner of the grey city she called home, there were many tight lines. She went and went until her veins frosted over. It was the first overdose that turned Emily into Blue.

When she saw him, the moon-eyed boy, he was Odin. He was the cyclops Polyphemus, tricked into believing in no one. He was Oedipus crazed and tortured and self-maimed. He was known to her somehow. Not for the eye itself but for the world that was lost behind it. The chunk of icecap sunken in seawater. Blue knew that a wound could also be a portal. That a wound could be a mouth, a lesson. A corridor of communication between souls. When she saw Blake Ackerman, she'd been clean for months and hadn't written down a thing. Her throat was hoarse and her mouth pill-dry. She hadn't thought about writing. She knew; somehow, she knew to follow him and talk to whatever gods lurked there. She knew to press her lips to his wound and holler.

CATHARTES-AURA

When the panther has eaten her fill, she lets out a great roar that seems to contain every scent. She is a beast marked with little circles of color like eyes. Her cubs scratch at the womb, prevented from being born. Animals with sharp claws cannot bear offspring because they are wounded internally by the movements of their young.

BLAKE

Maw always loved eating the heads of things. Sweet glee when fingering out an eyeball. The squelch of it. The smack of wet lips. When the earth turned black, food was always a problem. A constant argument in the home. How to preserve things, stew them in their own juices. How to endlessly cure and smoke the wild meat so that it would last us, though that also began to taste funny after a time and we all got the shits bad. After the cattle went, we ate goat on the regular. Somehow the wretchedness in those animals meant they could stomach the black earth just fine. Soups and stews that kept for weeks, stirred in with the leeks and onions. Thick beige broth and the whole house smelt of little kids boiling in a deep pan.

  We left Maw the heads. We didn't want them for ourselves—it scared us the way the eyes turned milky, blind and hollow. She used her tongue to fish out the sweetest parts, meat inside the cheek, and grinned at skulls as if comparing her smile to theirs. The sharp tug of her breath for the marrow made our ears pop. She threw the rest out for the dogs. After they were done, ants and beetles had their fun. Over the dinner table, I'd look at Jamie and he'd be staring at a point just above my head. His gaze would linger there, as if waiting for a movement, a small indication of life.

Vern took the skulls outside. Gathered them up in his arms. Tied them to low branches with stiff wire. Facing out and away. All had to face the Teeth, while Maw watched him from the porch nibbling at a hangnail. The goats kept a long eye on the mountain. Dotted around the house in uneven waves. Some higher up in the trees. Maw ate the heads to make sure they were gone forever. She said that if we didn't do that, if we didn't make sure things were truly dead—buried with the eyes facing down and the skulls turned away towards the mountain— they might come back for us. Growing up, the scuffling we heard in the tall grass when the wind blew hard, was all of those creatures dragging their bodies through the undergrowth towards us. All of those souls that weren't given a good enough burial needed to take us down with them. When the earth started turning black. When it started to smell and fester and our skins were crawling with worry. Folk started believing in the old ways and things that were once uttered with a smirk, batshit, irrational, ludicrous things were now recited as dogma, as fact, as the only explanation. Jamie never took his eyes off of that point above my head when we ate. Like Vern's hands working wire and bone. It tethered him in place.

I never minded churches. The large hollow space made me feel trapped inside a larynx. We'd had a metallic sculpture installed at the gallery, from floor to ceiling called Leviathan. All widgets and cardboard, ugly as hell. People winced and muttered underneath their breaths when they walked in to behold the monstrosity. It had speakers hidden inside its rib cage that spewed out field recordings of whale song gathered by a zoologist who followed pods of orcas around. He tried to map out their language through pinpointing specific patterns in their song that recurred. That large installation was an homage to everything he didn't understand about their ways. Workdays felt like being swallowed whole by a large marine animal.

The girl with the heavy-set jaw taught me things. I met her in a church. She was unlike anyone else in that way. She listened. She said it was fine to feel like death sometimes. Especially when mothers were involved and the past had its claws inside you. I viewed her as a short Amazon warrior with crushed sapphires for eyes. A tattoo in small font across her collarbone snarled: *Smooth your place among the wolves.* I had my spine rattled by her. She had problems too and was a natural with broken things. Blue. Blue got too much too early. Too much attention for a chronic introvert. By the end, she belly-flopped into the deep end of the pool and sank till her feet hit the bottom. Her poems were messy and wild, unique to those craving familiarity in the obscure. She had all of it memorized. I wished I could do that sometimes. I wished I could have her voice. At twenty-four, this was her second stretch after rehab. She ran AA meetings in churches like they were poetry workshops. All she seemed to care about was hearing all the voices at all times—stew-ing in that chorus.

'Volcanoes in a teardrop,' she shouted. 'Find two things that shouldn't work together but do. Nothing is wrong here. Don't think about it people. Whatever comes to you through glimpses. Waterfalls in a coffee-cup, a dragon with a hangover,' she said laughing, throwing her arms up over her head like she was summoning thousands of birds. Even then, I had a kind of love for her. A kind of dog's love when gnawing on a good bone. The addicts mumbled, tried out their long-lost tongues. She threw a light on all of them. Made them individuals. Made all of those caged birds sing with her sorcery. I sat with arms folded. There was a splinter in my big toe.

'Hold the pain in front of you,' she said pushing her hands out into space. 'Like a kind of balloon. Push into it with your palms and fingers. This is what you are hiding from, this is what you fear most of all in the world. Push hard but never let it burst.' I watched as they all stared into the empty space between their hands. All these track-marked manikins. Grey as goose feathers. The same solemn hymn tied us together. I unfolded my arms and the room quivered at the edges. My fingertips tingled with icy pins. Blood sat heavy in my stomach, rainwater in a bucket. My hands shook and were moist. They shook and my throat filled with tiny stones. I heard bark creaking. Smelled gasoline and a bitter muddy taste, earth and wood and slime under my tongue. Smell of the earth, foul, rotten. Bone through feather. A hoard of insects jostling bodies like puppets on the asphalt. The hole yawned next to me; a deep voice mumbled by my eardrum. Fumbled with a belt buckle, lower. I was all alone down there. All alone and up through the branches a red sky bore down. A lonely buzzard circled.

I inhaled sharply. The room faded back in. Without booze, there was no hiding. No hiding from how it all rose up out of nothing. At low temperatures, chaos takes on forms, structures, sculptures. It organizes itself for the eye to behold as something more than empti-ness, more than a blind spot. As I exhaled, the ceiling fan chirped and swung. Everyone dropped their hands, except me. I needed to hold it out there a little longer before it lunged back and claimed me whole. Chaos is a void that is alive still.

'How far can you push before it breaks?' Blue asked, looking us all up and down.

After the meeting, we stood on the church steps watching peo-ple drag themselves down the street. The girl with bleached cropped hair and a big jaw hung around. I noticed the inside of her fingers were tobacco stained. I pulled out my pack and we shared a smoke watching the road out front as everyone scattered and shuffled away. It took a couple of cigarettes more for her to start talking. Her head nodded at her boots as she took in my responses. As if retaining and holding each cadence. Blue looked deflated with only me left for an audience, her sapphires hidden behind thrift-store sunglasses. A threadbare sweater covering up a childhood of scoliosis. Her voice became smaller now that it was just the two of us.

'I think this is my last one of these,' she said, sniffing at an unlit cigarette.

'Really? What about the muddy coffees? The sights, the smells?' I said, threading another out, twisting it. She nodded at people leaving, huddled and shabby. Some had burst their pain balloons. Blue sucked her teeth. 'I will miss these broken marionettes. But I don't think I can give them back what they need. Not really,' she said bent over the banister in her baggy clothes, rubbing a hand through her hair. She flicked the filter until the tobacco fell out. I watched it dangling, like a large clump of hair about to fall from the scalp. There was a floral scent that came off her. Chemical, congealed washing powder in the creases of clothes. I realized that I hadn't been interested, impressed, or observant in this way of another perhaps since Harmswood—perhaps ever. Not like this. Not with this shimmering, like light through water. She sighed.

'I'm starting to wonder if any of this even works. If some of us are just born fucked. The wrong stuff in our veins. All of it tangled, sparks and snaps but no clean connection. Lately I've been thinking of death as a door,' she said swallowing. 'I keep having this dream that

'I'm walking barefoot in a forest. I'm still a kid, I can feel the shame of my body. Following something bigger up ahead of me. A big shaggy, grunting thing with horns and shoulders. The trees are mismatched. They slowly unravel and disperse into particles like birds. The soil becomes sinking sand. Blue hands drag me down into a kind of heat,' she said. I jangled my foot, pressed into the splinter until it broke the skin.

'When I wake up. At least when I think I've woken. Wolves sit at the foot of my bed. They wait and watch my breathing slow. Their muzzles hover over my toes. One by one they come at me. They tear me apart until all that is left burns until my eyes open,' she said and stared at me for a few moments. 'You look like you're holding a lot,' she said. 'I know about this new type of therapy they're trying. It triggers your memories and brings them all back in a new light. You don't just see the things that had happened but you feel them happening again and again until you accept the truth of it. It's the best and the worst and no amount of questions can replace feeling what really happened to you.' Blue said it was the only thing that helped her in the end. Before we knew it, it was nightfall. Streetlights budded open. Hours had passed. We were afraid to leave each other.

'Look, I'm into this thing. It involves tying people up—with rope. It might not be for you but why don't you come to the next show?'

'Like bondage?'

'It's like teasing out some freedom through constraint.'

It failed at first. All of it. The therapy, the meetings. I kept wak-ing up with a boulder crushing my chest. The mattress soaked through. The walls swirled behind a yellow curtain. The pain of not being able to see pain is excruciating.

BLUE

Summers in the gray city were a dry hump. Weather was close that time of year. The fuse on her fan burned out weeks back. A loud hiss in the night that made the teeth tingle. Sharp fumes in the nostril. She started leaving the refrigerator door open, stripped down to bra and boxer shorts. She'd hang one leg out the window, lean back against the frame trying to find the moon behind apartment blocks and antennas. No one interesting lived in the square rooms opposite. Through windows lit with TV screens, she'd never caught a glimpse of anything worthwhile. No flashes of flesh, no treats of skin. No one ever fucked. Especially not the young.

Blue was strict with herself. Rigid with routine. Cleaning up her act meant there was no swaying from the guided path. No more roads less travelled. She'd had to choose the smoothness of concrete over tangled roots. There was work. There were meetings. Something wrapped in plastic, crumpled inside foil; easy to heat up on the stove when she got home, easy to wolf down in an instant. Then of course, there was her prescription. A potent little assortment of milligrams to sustain all of that smoothness. A handful of pills, like quail eggs. No more distractions. No more love. Poems left her. They migrated in flocks. Made nests elsewhere. She turned her back on the thing that gave her weight in the world, that drew people to her, the royalties of which still paid her rent.

But when she got back after the last meeting, she didn't strip down to bra and boxers. She didn't open the fridge door and stare blankly into its large white mouth. No, she stood frozen in the middle of her apartment—fully clothed, eyes wired open. It came out of her pure. It burst through. After she got back home that night, there was a shift in things. Since going clean, she pretended her mind was a kind of exhibit. A room with furniture positioned at the right angle, the exact right distance between everything so that clutter made sense in her head. Space to breathe behind a thin membrane. Space to pretend and cool the tides down. She played in that negative space so that the wild was kept locked up inside a closet. Talking to the one-eyed Ozark boy had poked a small hole in the dam she'd built for herself. Now an impish feeling trickled out, sniffing the new air with delight and wonder.

A small red light blinked on her answer phone. Heaps of mes-sages. A windfall of them. She knew who from. She knew to let go of it. Every person in the world that showed interest was a harpy, a winged pest. All that heartache. All that bondage hadn't ended well. Blue ghosted Maureen when she saw the narcotic in her ways. She morphed herself around this person like clay and that's when it hit her that everyone she was close to was a kind of lost object. It wasn't them she wanted but how they filled in the gaps for what was never coming back, that which was forever deceased. Maureen had a good heart, a heart that needed to fix things. Blue met her through the BDSM scene. They played together for months, testing out each other's boundaries. Blue was immediately dominant, even though she'd never set that in-tention. The intensity of it fed the fight in her. She tied Maureen up in extended rough-play, they timed each other's orgasm, experiment-ed with spit and other juices. It was all safe for a time. All relatively mundane. Functional like a childish game; one counts to ten while the other hides.

Once, Maureen took the lead in the gentlest of ways. She wanted to play the dot and line game. Blue was on the floor with Maureen behind her. Cross-legged on the couch. In a hushed voice, Maureen began to whisper things to Blue. Her fingertips danced over the skin so that it pimpled. She drew a dot and then a line across each shoulder blade. Curled her fingers making them walk up and down the spine. She said it was a million spiders, she said it was millions of fish nibbling off the dead skin. *Spiders, spiders, spiders,* her fingertips whispered, *fish, fish, fish.* The more she whispered, the more Blue felt herself gliding into the swarm and being devoured by all the little hungry mouths. Maureen then cupped both hands high and pretended to crack an egg on Blue's skull and, with open palms, she mimicked the motion of yolk sliding down to the small of her back. It was this feeling, this moment, the lack and loss of control, giving up her force, her mind and her shape in the world to the formlessness of oblivion that killed it for her. It was that hateful trust which turned love into opium. For that, she had to shut it down. That tingling meant things. That lava glow held her too tightly. That intimacy led to obsession, to gluttony. The little red light, with its trapped chorus of voices was a winking fascist.

No more love; but Blue didn't enjoy it. She hated every second of being cold. Of not fully adopting and falling into the arms of the other. Every second was a reminder of what not to do, of what not to be. After rehab, her life was about not being everything she felt she was. Burning up the origami birds of her consciousness. Living with the taste of their ashes in her mouth. She stood there in the middle of her cramped apartment and for the first time, felt like she needed more than a flatline to pull her through the night. She walked to the bathroom and opened the mirror-cabinet. Little plastic containers sat in a row. Her equalizers. Stabilizers. Dumb-downers. Sex-killers. All she needed to keep her alive and sleeping. She envisioned the cascade of white pills as an avalanche, a blizzard blocking her sight. It all crystallized in the action of her flushing them away. Clarity. Down and down, they swirled, expelled into the gutter for the rats and the roaches and the mythical mole-people. Her skin crawled with it; her heart blew up inside her throat. How wrong it was, how great it felt, how the exile of being medicated had groomed her into a waking hibernation. She thought that perhaps this injection of antidepressants might sedate the tides of the sewers beneath the gray city, that it might bring bliss to the mange-ridden. With pills now swirling beneath her feet, she searched high and low for her notepad. A pen, pencil, a piece of charcoal—anything to get it down after all this time. She found a long supermarket receipt and a small blue pen, dry at the tip. A pause. A breath. A whisper. There it was; happening in jagged and unhappy handwriting. She scribbled it down as it came to her. It was new. A new version of herself. A voice that hadn't exposed itself before that very moment. And somehow it was connected to that boy's fucked eye, his cracked core, how his laugh was more of a wince, every breath a sigh of embarrassment. A person so loudly haunted. She wrote as if speaking to him, for him. For the voice he didn't have. Out it spilled until her little blunt pen tore the receipt a new asshole and she continued onto the desk tearing lines through fresh words and starting over until she had two paragraphs—two pieces of herself mined and spun from the ether. Dream pieces, black magic. These were conjured words and they came from a feeling in the gut after speaking to the one-eyed Ozark boy.

'You used to think the nights were made of panthers. That they stalked you. That you lived to be stalked. Sometimes you'll be sitting, thinking. Pacing back and forth in your apartment, or walking down the street for cigarettes. The air will sometimes smell of daphne and honeysuckle. As you walk you will see all the animals merge. Not emerge, but sort of be in the frame. Pushed out from the center to the periphery. A whole pride of panthers make up the night.

'You will be distracted by a limb or tail hanging down from a roof. By the possibility of a big cat rolling around playfully in shad-ows—shadows that are her and she them. When someone catches a heel on the sidewalk, it is a sound that could just as easily be a dog in pain. There is always a panther prowling. You used to think the nights were made of panthers. That you lived to be stalked.'

Her fingers were smudged with ink. Cramping like claws. She didn't know what it meant. If someone were to ask her, she'd rather be punched square in the nose than attempt to decipher it. All she knew was that it heightened her. It was both of and from a real place. It was the first time in a long time that Blue didn't care that she couldn't see the moon, hidden away for row upon row of lifeless apartment blocks. If she squinted up through the mesh of artificial light, she swore she could see the roaming, prowling figures of big cats on the rooftops, criss-crossing each other.

CATHARTES-AURA

Tap, tap, tap.

BLAKE

There are certain things that end up owning your heart. It started a few months into knowing each other and it was bad at first. We had no clue how to move, how to read each other's body. But the understanding was there, always the urge. She tied the rope in knots over me like a harness. Hogtied. Held my neck in both her hands, thumbs into my windpipe. When she let go, our skins rippled. Walls of red and black everywhere. We took freezing showers after that burned us alive, so we could start anew.

'Choke me,' I would plead as she began easing the Bald-Knob out of me, only for a few moments. We both needed something of each other in this way. We had an understanding. We became the wilder-ness. We were freed. The world was a Rothko painting.

It started after the first rope show. It started after sessions with the therapist and her light and her soft-voiced questions. Blue took me there to get fixed. I was doing the method that had helped her. Mov-ing my eyes from side to side. Following a light that hurt me. Little by little, I found myself falling, falling into places I never thought I'd go. Blue made the whole thing possible. For the longest time, I was mute. That's the first thing that hit; voicelessness. If I didn't say it, it didn't happen. I swallowed all those wrong words, those filthy words like mouthfuls of soil and let the Bald-Knob gorge. But the past goes nowhere but inwards, burrowing in deeper like a scared rat. Little by little. The ice melted until I felt my body as a child. Rough hands in small places. Always a musk hanging in the air. Man's musk. Maps nev-er meet dead ends, only monsters, maws, freaks and fiends.

Blue was part of a kink-crew. They all tied each other up. Suspended themselves from wooden frames with hooks in the ceiling. Teased and tormented each other with both softness and strength. It took courage and control. Two at a time, tied. One wrapped the other in beautiful knots, as if they'd been caught in a fishing net, yanked mer-people. It had love somewhere inside it, it had a big heart. She took me to the basement of a dingy bar in the city. Invited into her world, where she was responsible for my behavior, and I liked it. I liked the control she had. As we descended, I clutched a tepid ginger beer to my chest. Blue kept looking back to reassure, she pulled me along by my sleeve.

It was packed and steamy. Rows of seats and throbbing bass-heavy music. Couples in leather jackets holding hands. Balding men with ponytails. Tattoos of grimacing pumpkins, cobwebs and other horror-themed images crawled all the way up their arms. It smelt stagnant. The people looked normal enough to be anyone. Underneath the paraphernalia, they were computer technicians, retail assistants, they were us. All of them knew Blue. A girl in a translucent gown and red brassiere ran up from across the room kissed her on both cheeks, hugged her close. She was the organizer. Blue looked stiff. I couldn't hear what they were saying over the loud boom of bass and kick drum, the lights made me feel epileptic, my thoughts were splitting like fig skins. But I liked it, I liked being there and not at home nibbling on hangnails and chain smoking.

'Where've you been, beautiful?' I heard the brassiere girl say.

Blue nodded, shooting me embarrassed glances. She twisted her lips, picked at the end of her chin. I felt warm with Blue. I could follow her anywhere. The organizer didn't look at me once. It was like her long-lost leader had emerged from the desert. She had no time for whatever the cat dragged in behind her. We sat down cross-legged at the front next to the stage. Two spotlights fell on a wooden structure, like gallows. A beam supported by two triangular fixtures on either side. Thick ropes lay bundled in four corners on the floor.

'They're really excited about this,' Blue whispered in my ear. 'It's their first official showcase,' she said.

'They seem to love you,' I said.

'What?' said Blue distracted by noise, the lights, her people.

'I said it looks like they really appreciate you being here,' editing myself.

'Well, I used to be pretty involved for a while. Kind of like a family to me when I first got sober. We would hang out at each other's houses and start tying each other, playing. It was awesome. Then I got into a relationship and she wasn't cool with me being tied, coming home black and blue. She didn't understand what it meant for me. So, I disappeared on these guys for a long time. Then we broke up and I fell off the wagon, you know the rest. I've just started tying again. But it's like riding a bike,' she said and pulled her beanie off her head. 'Anyhow, I thought you might get something out of it,'. I gestured with my bottle and the music stopped. A couple had been sitting in the shadows by the installation. A man and woman. He was tall, lanky. Shaved head, corvid. She was in a thin flannel dress leaning into his chest. They were both staring at the floor when the lights fell on them.

'That's Juan,' whispered Blue, as they were being introduced to the crowd. 'He set up this whole thing from day one. He weaves his own ropes and everything.' 'Who's she?' I asked. But it began and everything in me tensed up. The music shifted. Became atonal. Something cold-blooded treading on cello strings. The two figures stood up and stepped into the light. She knelt down in her pretty white dress, hands folded into her lap, head tilted to an angle. Juan was behind her in the shadows preparing the ropes. He pulled a hood over his head and pushed a mask over his nose and mouth, like a plague doctor. Then it was happening. Flurries. Whips of rope as he twisted and looped them around her small body, almost childlike, cherubim. I could hear his breathing as it closed in on her, heavier each time he added a new layer. As the rope rubbed against itself, it sounded like fire cracking the pines open. The rope was the whole forest up in flames—it was bones falling through space, splintering on cold blue stones. It made me think of when they used to burn the rim of the woods in late summer, to keep the deer ticks down and allow things to grow through the ashes, stronger, full of rage.

There was something in it. Something about how they did it to each other, a delicate ferocity in the fingers. The consistency of flesh as it pushed out through the gaps. Pleasure, pain, connection. She hung, suspended. He twirled her around and I saw the rope push into her thighs, under the armpits and breasts. I saw the transformation brought on by a specific kind of pain. As he moved around her, she whispered subtle instructions. Where things hurt too bad. He molded the flesh around the rope so that she felt at ease in their dance. A film was projected behind them in black and white, a small child running with its back to us. I felt Blue next to me. Fully present. Fully embodied. The running child worried me. The tightening of the rope worried me. The dissonance in the music filed my focus down to a sharp tooth. The girl groaned. Juan was transfixed by what he had at hand. By what the world was letting him do in this basement in front of all these people that applauded him. Who called him talented, who called him an artist, a craftsman, a god. I could only see the child running.

He twirled her. Twisted her around. The sounds emanating from her pressed like knuckles into my panic attack. That little man on fire running around inside me. The kid running in sequence, slide after slide. Dry-throat, a pressure behind the eyes. I swirled as she swirled like a happy fly. Kicking, words kicking, each vibration like a whip. Ropes smacking hard on the concrete. Finger-plucked violin through speakers. The Bald-Knob launched himself against the door, head first. His one wing too large for the small staircase. I'd left him alone out there. I thought I could handle it with Blue by my side. The girl was horizontal now, ankles and wrists bunched together like flowers. A buck in deer-season.

Tightening and twisting. Something whistled. Whistled in the tall grass. Whistled through the air and pierced my face before I could fully see. She groaned like goats in a slaughterhouse, like watching Vern cut things off and sear the wound shut with hot metal. Close to forty-five minutes in, I closed my good eye. The Bald-Knob kept slamming himself into the door, the walls, he threw up on himself out of fear—he knew what was coming and couldn't stop it. I don't know why, but I thought the rope might sing to me, over her body.

It was over. The music stopped. The projector switched off.

Clapping. Cheering. The child stopped running. Collapsed into the black screen. They sat there on the floor in their nest of ropes, in an embrace. He held her from behind, nuzzled into her neck saying things that only a person who truly knew her could mouth. She was luminous, higher than anything. Her face a plate of light. But I was not there. I was in the woods, with the dark bark creaking. Again and again, I was on my back. Boots around me, the weight of men's words. It wasn't just Maw that was caught in the Teeth. When I opened my good eye, out fell a waterfall. Spewed out of me and I shook with fury, rage that looked weak but felt like wild horses. The clapping, the cheering covered me as I wept. The two artists were happy, smiling—alive.

Blue saw me in that moment. Truly saw me and, for that, she owned my heart.

BLUE

When she wrote about him, she wrote about herself:

You started drinking early. Still stinging from botched eye surgeries. She'd let you dip a finger in and swirl it around. You sucked it dry like an ice-pop. The edges of wallpaper shimmered. The pipes groaned through the walls. The wound stung less. Sang less. There was a difference between the day and the night in the house you grew up in, in the town you grew up in. The night had a warm wetness some-where further down after the lights went out. Damp breath on your faces the color of liquor. Stories carried you off, through a crack in the window, through beating wings and hissing sounds. Plucked you off the ground. You climbed that scaffolding of words. The days hurt, the nights swirled. You sipped and sipped until the records stopped play-ing. A fifth of whiskey. You chained yourself to a rock for scavengers.

The worst thing to do is feed your addiction. That's what they say, those that have known the laughing snake. Don't feed your de-mons. Soon as you've downed one glass, it all becomes a funnel at-tached to a dirty ocean. One then another until the end of the world feels like a small dot. Plugging holes in a fishing boat. You could hardly remember yourself most days, most days were yellow and frayed at the ends. Clawed out. At what point did she become the wilderness. She was a vegetable for a good while before she passed. You said your uncle was somber on the phone like nothing much happened. Her twin. You said his voice was rinsed like top soil after a bushfire and I didn't under-stand. She went in the night, you said. You didn't go to your mother's funeral. You dreamt of her eyes wide open.

THERAPY

Tap, tap, tap.

That sound that had always folded my face into a pillow. Be-tween the heat of headphones. The sting of my eye that pushed against sleep and my back turned to the windowpane. There wasn't an end to that memory, it traveled in a circle. The therapist had a soft voice. She started adding on endings. Adding on words. Pruning down the wild to get to the source. She said she could see it on me, all of it. That it was loud. At the beginning of each session, she would say that sometimes we live in the shadow of an object we can't see. A hoof, a paw, a wingspan. I thought of the Teeth, how they were always in our sight. Always watching. How those mountains were the shape of every thought. Patient and ancient. How for eighteen years I saw those three canines pushing up into soft flesh of heaven.

Tap, tap, tap.

The more endings she added, the more they explained almost everything. Almost. They explained why the night wouldn't let me sleep sober, why I had a turkey-vulture in the corner of my mind al-ways. Why he had a name. Why I could never speak that name. That he was a symbol of home and loss and shame and crooked love. That all he was, ultimately, a defense mechanism. She fished it out of me in that disarming quiet. At first, it was crystallized inside an image of the dream I'd had as a kid stuck between a scorched field and the forest unfolding like tentacles. Tapping in the silent room. Tapping on glass. Tapping, until my own fingers matched it on the table as she spoke and I answered. The light swinging in front of me morphed into a body as I talked.

A boy's body. Wilf Batty came back to me and I finally saw. I saw him looking at me with his wood-pigeon doll. Body in one hand. Head in the other. The head fell off and rolled all the way up to my feet. I saw naked bodies stacked on top of each other in a field. Smoth-ered in moonlight. Working away, blessing the earth. I heard gurgling, moaning. I had visions.

Through the body of light, I heard folk talking about Batty. I picked at the cacophony of conversations that swirled around my head. His name bounced between the walls in my house. I had a soft spot for the slow boy, the loggerhead. There was a sweetness. A pure kind of knowing. His folks were too old for such a young kid. We heard things after he died, you couldn't avoid it no matter what. So much unsaid in my hometown. Naked bodies in the moonlight. I kept seeing them over and over in that swinging bulb. Swarming the fields. Digging, dancing, fornicating in the soil. I kept hearing the bedroom window open and shut again. Jamie's body floating through the air. But was it real? Was it true? It nibbled at my feet. The therapist told me to trust.

Tap, tap, tap.

Wilf couldn't talk well. I always remembered that. Called me 'Yyyyake', my name drawn out like a mating call. Smiling, rocking on his feet. Squinting like he always had sun in his eyes.

'I seen Howlers, Yyyyake. I seen 'em,' like he was talking from behind a wall, cemented. He never scared me. He was just touched. He ran away from home a few times and they had to nail his window shut so he wouldn't leave. He wanted to get back to the woods. Once, he'd gone missing for a day and a half, till some logger found him half soaked to death under a bridge after having swum the creek, with the biggest smile, ear to ear. They said Wilf was found as a baby bundled under the tree line, raccoons prodding his cheeks. His Mama swore he was hers, that it was a miracle, even though she was well beyond her childbearing years.

Tap, tap, tap.

The therapist made me follow her finger. I gagged in my first session. Clutched at my throat. I felt Vern push rags into my mouth. It made the voice fade and little white dots appear in front of me. The drinking was only the beginning, there was more waiting to come out. A sleeping truth, like bears. I'd tried other shrinks but their questions were wrong. Their questions were objects thrown down a well. If I didn't say it, it never happened. The Bald-Knob hissed and fanned out his pinion but the boy was still alive and couldn't be silenced. Alive but chained up to the pain. My creation story started with an ending. In a whisper of hot breath on the neck. The musk that stained my body. Manure and early morning. With a carrion bird pushed aside, I watched my past ignite from some sunken place. Many times, I ended up on the floor. Trying to shove two fists in my mouth and stop words meeting with the air.

But the soft voice burrowed in further. More endings. It came for me from above. All the way down to where I had been sleeping since childhood. Her voice flew lower and lower, trying to get where it needed to be. It tried to make me see through the black feathers, pushed the Bald-Knob off of me, his beak all bloodied. Each time I got closer, my body remembered a little bit more. In my eye and else-where, somewhere lower—where weeds grew and cobwebs formed. It hummed louder and louder. The light swelled until I started to see what was happening behind it.

Before I could get through to the other side and touch that child again. Before I felt anything real, there was everything else to reconcile. There was a wall of text. Books kept me alive for so long. They gave my life meaning. I learned to cry in that little dark room, weeping that grew from tapping dragon scales, from clutching the red leaves of that fall. I had become so good at hiding.

Everything under the surface is red. Red under the skin, under the earth, behind the eyelids. Red is the hidden truth. I never ques-tioned my uncle. I never asked what we were doing all those times driving back and forth with something hammering away in the trunk. Never asked why I was the only one he trusted to take out there. I tast-ed it; huffing on a damp rag, chewing on the sour tang of mushrooms. All twisted up from day one. Tap, tap tap—like a machine my fingers danced. Tap, tap, tap—typewriter keys. Tap, tap, tap—fingers on the windowpane. Howlers. Wilf. Jamie. All the things I couldn't see were in that fucking sound, in that tapping. Trapped in a fingertip memory.

What would I tell my brother? What would I tell the boy that was now a man, about what really happened? What would I say to the bastard? The wildcat I abandoned when I got on the greyhound, watching the trees grow small. I was a mess after each session. I wanted liquor but got Blue instead. A burger and a cigarette. It crushed me to know the truth of it, but you have to sink before you float. The ghosts of my six dead dogs ran after me down the asphalt. I was Odin because Odin had one eye. He sacrificed his sight so that he might see. Blue's ropes and the soft voice pulled me out of the mire. They saved me.

'Yyyyake?' asked Batty, from the black box behind my skull. In the end, I realized that some of us kids were just offerings.

BLUE

She spun outwardly. Spun like a spider on acid, as the glass pane of sobriety started to form cracks. The writing caught fire. Everything caught fire. She knew that this was the truth of it, no pills, no talking but a pure long drag on the fumes of those words as they raced ahead of her into the deep. Suddenly her dull little apartment was full of color, movement and fleshy glimpses. Suddenly the walls shouted rhymes and thoughts from post-it notes. When she spoke to him, she spoke to herself also. Words on the page were ants at work on a carcass:

The world that walks inside you might walk away. You tug at your zipper in the autumn chill, fingers are a language. Your dark cir-cles are a language, but you see me in a way that others don't. As I see Pan sitting on your chest, Blake. I see how much he mocks you lying there caught under his hoof, Blake. You pull the zipper all the way up to your throat, hunch your shoulders against the cold. There is some-thing of the fighting dog about you, a broad-backed, thick-skinned thing. Funny how all it takes is a slit for the light to get in. The rip of a claw. You fall through pine and soil, through a man's wet breath, on your back again under the sky, shaking.

Serpent.

Mouth.

Tail.

Tail.

Mouth.

Serpent.

Blue felt the dot and then the line drawn. She felt the spider and the fish on her skin. She felt the large Orphic egg crack and the serpent uncoil within.

CATHARTES-AURA

Maenads ran around the countryside tearing apart animals and children. But they were not intoxicated solely on wine. Amanita Muscaria induces hallucinations, senseless rioting, prophetic sight, erotic energy, and muscular strength. It was ingested by Norse berserkers to give them ferocity in battle.

BLAKE

The Ozark Howler wasn't a big black cat and he wasn't a winged moose with glowing red eyes. He was what everyone thought lived in the darkness. He was what people feared most in themselves. A ghost from a crypt in the mind. He was what was breathed out after generations of inhaled violence. A lived-in neglect. He was Vern. My uncle worked on his kids. Bucks were to be dehorned and castrated. Jamie and I watched this sometimes. The hiss. The smell, always the smell lingered. They'd had us believe that we were all split into two perfect versions: light and dark, moon and sun, male and female—dualities only. That's what gets tattooed on the skins of the young. People didn't feel comfortable in the gray, the static that ran through and under it all. I remember because my clothes smelled thickly of fire, always. I had to leave. I had to run. Leave Maw her growing pains and night terrors. Clutching one of her breasts and looking away as if I'd stabbed her. That last image.

Once, we'd gone fishing. Three of us in a boat out on the lake. Jamie wasn't hooking the worms right. I watched the water as they shouted at each other. We'd been out there since dawn when, finally, the line pulled and almost tipped us. It cut deep into our palms. Vern gave it all he had and hoisted out an eel the length of a small man. It fell over us thrashing, eyes flat as discs. Vern pushed the prehistoric head down with his boot but it broke loose and bit between his thumb and forefinger with a bear-trap mouth that kept closing. It was Jamie who acted. While I watched frozen, he clambered through and unsheathed a knife from Vern's belt. Pushed the blade deep into a slit in the gills until the eyes emptied. I was paralyzed by how something so scary could live beneath lily pads, coots, and frogspawn. It released its bite, softened into a heap. Jamie pulled the knife all the way down. A hint of rainbow spilled from the animal, colors in a storm. My brother was covered in fish guts, staring down at them. The bite mark on Vern's hand turned white in later years. I was too sure the little wildcat would grow up into a whisky-barreled alligator man that couldn't be put down.

Vern gave me that knife, with its small antler handle. Even though it should've been Jamie's. He gave me it to me for keeping a secret. I was never good with my hands but I liked the stories I could weave from the knife. The deer; before it was turned into an object, whitetail or elk. The sinkhole in the middle of the forest is where we dumped waste. Refrigerators, tractor engines, furniture full of woodworm. The creek washed it down. Down into the underworld. It was out beyond the water tower. A dirt path carved by God's broken fingernails. A half hour trek with a wheelbarrow. Deeper and deeper until you couldn't see. I once asked Vern why we threw the dogs down there.

'We don't need them no more. But *they* might,' is all he said.

I didn't know that Jamie went there alone. There was a clearing around the sinkhole, where it had eaten everything up. No trees, no greenery. The cleanest mountain water in the filthiest places, it was good to drink and made us feel better than we were. The pull of myth was louder out there. Inside me, a cornucopia of little mouths waiting to be fed by text, words as nutrition. But beyond that, I knew of nothing else. I developed tunnel vision, ignored the movements on either side of my consciousness. No matter what, as long as I had my uncle to cut back the branches, I was safe. I followed his instructions and we went deeper. When I couldn't see, I clung to his belt.

'All paths lead to Rome,' he said and whistled strangely the deeper we went. The sinkhole was one of his favorite spots. So many stories about how lonely the Devil was in Arkansas. He called the sinkhole Old Luce. We fooled around when we got there. Threatened to throw each other in. Dipped a toe, then a foot, then a limb and then all of ourselves. The more body parts were submerged the braver. Vern watched me twirling on the brink, he even laughed some.

'That's where God puts all the bad folk so not even the buzzards can get them. How bad are you, I wonder?' he said.

Each year, the rains came. Dust turned to mud. I saw fat tails. Emotions like mud dragons, horned shells, lidless eyes. Vern stood behind me as we watched everything sink. Old Luce gobbled it all up. The stench of Marlboros Reds cocooned my head. Bubbles bloomed and popped like frog's eyes. The first time was after our sixth dog died. Vern gave me a rag. Told me to breathe in. I did it until everything slipped from my eye like a fat tear. Tree trunks erupted. The many tips of flame. He ripped out a handful of mushrooms from a log and I huffed. They seemed to be leaking through his hands like raw eggs.

Brown with orange frills, they should've been at the bottom of the ocean growing next to a whale's eyeball. He took the rag away and pushed a couple into my mouth, held my jaw shut until I swallowed. He said it was medicine, that we shouldn't go in this deep without it. I felt sicker than anything, but kept it all down.

He took the rag away. Shoved it in his back pocket and slowly laid me down. I felt a swell, a vibration. The sky was geometric wallpaper. Raw but blunt between my legs. My lips were wet. I looked to my side and the sinkhole was moving like a mouth, trying to talk to me. After that, it's hard to know really. It became ritual. In the woods, we made things disappear. A whisper in my ear said 'If you ever tell on me, Old Luce'll have your bones.' When I looked into the trees, every bird flew out at once. Some things just couldn't be swallowed whole. They got caught up in the Teeth. This was only the beginning, the squirt from a whale's blowhole, the tail fins before it dove under. I needed to stay with Old Luce before she disappeared.

The Bald-Knob was perched a few yards away, further and further.

BLUE

There is life. Just on the other side of this. Blue talked to Blake about the god with blue balls. The god of shepherds. Her poems were full of him clicking his tongue, scratching his nether regions. She wanted Blake to see her polish the low hanging testicles until they shone, to hold them in her hands like bird eggs. She wanted him to see her crack the panic open. To see her shove her face deep into its leg fur and inhale the weather that seeped into his wool. To show him that fear is filthy. Fear locked her jaw. Blue needed him to know that the blue-balled god never stole her voice.

CATHARTES AURA

This you can't unsee.

BLAKE

Laundry helped. Little tasks. Something I could measure. Something I could count on my fingers and toes. God drummed his fingers. I hadn't left the apartment in days. Plates and take-away boxes piled up, threatening to topple over. I lived under a blanket. Sores inside my cheek from biting, ulcers coated my throat, sweat in sheets over the brow. Maw died like I knew she would. Maw died but it didn't matter anymore. I imagined her going out swinging a knife at an oncoming storm, 'I'll cut you here. I'll cut you there.' She used to say that to me when we played butcher-shop. It felt sort of ticklish as I lay down on the couch, or the bed, or the floor and she stooped over me, and flattened her palm into a blade. She asked me what she should sever next, stopping at my crotch and sort of smiling to herself. 'What's this, birdie?' she'd say, prodding. As if one swift cut could rid the world of all its evils. I imagined her wading through that field, in her nightgown, raging against that storm.

The light swung. The rope spoke. I had seen it now; the truth of it. They called it abuse. I called it witchcraft. That's what you called things you didn't understand. Devils, unknowns. They could've killed us on the wrong day. Tapping on the side of my brain, on the windowpane. Maw died and I still kept her scream in my marrow. I bet they never gave her that dying wish. I bet Vern had a hard-on for his sudden power to choose what happened to her. Or perhaps it all just went in the end. I had trouble picturing my uncle as the light swung. He was a big man, large broad and muscular with a high voice, he talked as if in a trance with his head tilted back. Faces in space, in drapes, in raindrops, on glass. Mouths that devoured each other. Head inside mouth.

I tried to sweep Jamie away. I tried, but he was seeded deep into the soil of me. He sat in a web at the back of my head like a large fat spider. Older brothers are supposed to protect their siblings. I used to feel the world with him when Maw let me outside. We'd walk along kicking up ant hills. They opened and we watched all the souls escaping. I'd feel pity for the little insects, but he kicked more viciously, more violently than me. We were the ants. We were the strange lights in the sky, the things everyone ignored. In spring, Vern gelded bullocks. They moaned, oblivious as he heated the blade. We saw their immortality torn from the root. Tossed into a corner like a handful of beets.

'If he doesn't do it, the cows will turn on us. They'll trample the house down looking for us,' Jamie said when he saw my eyes were full of water, my cheeks puffed red. Vern heard him whispering and caught us. Smirked, called us soft and pointed the glowing knife at my brother. Jamie's heart was big, like Blue's. They shared a lot, my brother with this strange girl. She'd been calling. Every day since the last therapy session. I turned my phone over until the buzzing stopped. I turned it back up to see my face in the black mirror. Promised myself I'd call back, after the laundry was done. First, I wanted to watch all of it churning over. I wanted to watch the rot flushed out.

After therapy, I felt that all my books were liars. I wanted to sew their mouths shut. I wanted to live inside a white void. I looked at them with a kind of shame from under the blanket, piled up in limp dusty towers. My phone lit up and died down again. Books were the raised platforms on which I was placed as a boy. Platforms that saved me from the wild. I couldn't hate them for too long. The Bald-Knob turned his head to look at me, crestfallen. He was looking rough, withered, out of touch with me. I pushed myself up from the knees. Cartilage, rubbing on something harder. Knowing – Changes – Everything. An acorn dropped into a puddle from a great height spreading its circles wide. I stepped over piles of unwashed clothes and opened the fridge to a small plate of chicken bones, strands of darkened meat hanging off them. Chicken skin congeals after a few hours. The cold made it thicker, chewier. I sucked out all the marrow, cracked each thin bone wide open. Two, three days old—the cold kills decay—I took the plate and cracked more bones with my teeth. The marrow was still good to eat, the best part of the bird.

I sucked it all out through the wishbone, sucked so hard like I was waiting for it to become an instrument. The meat was cool in my mouth. Thoughts fluttered. My brain was a battery dying in a flashlight. Shattering up against the night sky. Animals waiting in the distance. Animals changed in the dark like everything else does. There was a large white sign in the middle of our family plot, God knows who put it there. It had always been blank, a large white surface like a lighthouse or the moon. I'd fallen underneath it once while riding a bike. I looked up and four spray painted letters loomed large, for the first time. The word was SOON. It could have been a dream. My phone buzzed again, clinking against the plate of chicken bones. Blue again. I needed to hold on to what mattered. Soon, after all, might be too late.

After the last session, Blue and I sat in silence. The world rolled by in strollers pushed along by tired mothers, dragged down by their creations. A horn beeped, someone cursed, a couple tied its tongue into knots. I rubbed my hands down my legs. Up again, down again, up again. A tightness that wouldn't go away, the frog in my throat kicked, a kind of magic inside it all. As we sat on a bench, Blue drew her knees up to her chin, twirling a lit cigarette like a propeller. She waited for the full hour.

'So, any good?' she said.

'Panic attacks,' I said, a little on the quiet side. 'Makes me nauseous. Makes me see a lot of things.'

'What are you going to do about it?' she said. I didn't answer. Just stared at the young couple eating each other alive.

'You will remember this,' she said. I got that feeling. That blue-black space in the cavity of my chest. Pulling everything in the world down. That dryness in the throat. I got up and dry-heaved into a bin. Then I said something vague and power-walked away, leaving her. Street after street, crossing, waiting. It took everything I had not to patronize every bar in the universe. Key. Unlock. Inside. Inside. Inside. We hadn't talked since.

'Blue?' I picked up.

'I thought you died, you asshole,' she said. A pause.

'It's good to hear your voice, buddy,' I said.

'You haven't called. I figured maybe it was all too much. Maybe you needed pacing out slower. The rope was kind of wild, and then therapy. Sorry if I pushed you,' she said and I could hear her biting her sleeve with her teeth.

'There's so much I can only justify with a feeling. If justify is the right word. Before all of this I wasn't even sure I was alive,' I said. I swore I heard her eyes roll upward through the receiver.

'Stop looking for the right words,' she said. 'Looking for the right words is what got me smoking junk at house parties. Looking for the right words is what killed the right words. Forget the right words, Blake. You feel what you feel,' she said.

Blue was right. The phone burned against my head like a hot coal. We both breathed into the mouthpiece from opposite ends. I thought of one tree in a sea of trees. All the manifestations of a cracked mind walked between them. What was that one tree in a sea of trees doing, that thin sapling that scaled and measured the world year after year, reaching up to claw the heavens open. Blue was seeing it with me. Always with me, even when I was a child in the middle of nowhere. With me somehow, as my brain unfurled into a murmuration of star-lings. I so loved it. I still loved it.

Wilf Batty was strong. Even before he died. Before the monsters caught him and did what monsters do. I believe he took death in a way that no one else could, until pupil dilated over iris. I believe the song of his silence nearly ended those beasts, nearly broke their black hearts open like peach pits. No one believed we found him; he wasn't where we said he was. Just me bleeding out of my face and my brother crying.

'Blue?' I said.

'Yes?' she said.

'I think I want to feel everything now,' I said. 'I think I want to feel everything. Can you tie me?' 'Yes,' she said.

BLUE

He had a theory about what these Howlers were. That the gods were all-animal. He kept a newspaper clipping from way back. Showed her it. It said apes had escaped from a testing lab outside his hometown. Large dangerous apes they called man-killers broke out of their cages. He said the bigger boys were taken out of school to go monkey hunting. They caused havoc and mauled some woman's face off. All of them escaped. Ran hobbling and loping across the asphalt, into the fields, towards the pines. He said rumor had it they were never caught. He said they were left alone to breed up there in the caves, down in the mine shafts. That they left folk alone for a small price. He had the newspaper clipping folded up in one of his journals that looked fake as hell. A black and white photograph of hulking figures in the rye. Gorilla-costumed fools. Blue liked the reality of him believing it. That there might be wild apes on the loose in Arkansas causing all that trouble, all that havoc, all that heartache.

CATHARTES-AURA

Pan was rejected by the nymph Syrinx and so he turned her into reeds for his pipes. Birdsong comes from an organ in throat called the syrinx.

Buzzards lack this organ.

They lack song.

BLAKE

There was a cinema beneath my apartment. It played silent films. I could sometimes hear the hum of the projector. Flashing lights from under the floorboards. It was a good way to spend the night, laid out on the floor, like a skinned tiger. I'd press my ear down and listen to crunching popcorn. Couples in their seats. Fingers twisting in each other's hair. I asked Blue to come by and tie me after her shift. I couldn't get it out of my head. How they managed to turn pain into an art form, into sex, into anything in the world they wanted. To transpose darkness into light through the tightening of a rope. It felt vital. It scraped every nerve inside me as I watched that girl rotate in her ripped white dress with cornflower blue ducklings embroidered over it. Distended from the ceiling, dressed out, ecstatic and milky eyed. I asked Blue to tie me because I needed to taste the security in that abandon.

    I buzzed her in. I threw plates into garbage bags and ran

through my two rooms swirling cans of air-freshener. I opened a window to let in police sirens and wailing cats as she climbed the stairs to mine. There was a janitor in my building that stared too long. The nail on his pinky left to grow for slicing cigarette packs open. I hoped Blue hadn't seen him lurking, hadn't seen the overgrown nail. She had to climb through an underworld. I opened up. She stood there, hooded and pale. A backpack full of ropes. Warmth washed over me. Days since I'd seen her last only to realize how stupid it was to push her away. There was literally no one else left in the world for me but Blue. Blue and this new way of seeing, of feeling. She nodded. Brushed past me. I shut the door.

She pushed books and loose papers off my coffee table, kneeled, and emptied the contents of her bag. Placed three sets of rope next to each other. Black, olive and deep maroon. She sat back and studied each with focus. Eyeballs that bounced from one object to the next. I traced the line of her collarbone, each tattooed word and the image it conjured. Smooth. Place. Wolves. A small white scar where they burnt out a mole; a moon for those wolves. Blue embodied her poetry, lived it. She picked the olive bunch and began unwinding it, sprawling it out in patterns if she were about read the entrails of a sacrifice. I hovered over her shoulder. Lit candles. The shaky light turned my furniture into an arctic landscape.

It was her calm that held me. The way she handled everything with strong delicate fingers. She didn't flinch, she didn't wish she was somewhere else. Throughout my life I hadn't known much of that. Only books listened. Whenever I was on a binge, there'd be a sadness somewhere in my chest, a deep hollow. Endless falling. Bottomless no matter what I poured down it. A sadness for the world and every person in it opened its wings but got stuck between head and heart, ricocheting. The memories were organs growing back. In the beginning there was no image, just figures, texture, grainy like salted skin. Just that feeling of sadness that always grew back. I placed these new organs in Blue's hands. So she could read them. So she could handle them, with strong delicate fingers.

'Strip down,' she said. I did as I was told. Pulled my sweater off, painfully aware of my body. How my ribs protruded. The big painful pimple on my back I couldn't reach. My body was shapeless as I stood there in my thin boxer shorts. She organized the ropes whispering under her breath, guiding herself through the motions. Not a care in the world for what I looked like.

'Kneel here,' she said pointing to the middle of the carpet. We settled into our positions. She gathered the ropes. I was her snared rabbit, a bunny, control handed over. She prowled around psyching herself up, trying to remember each step to the dance. I heard her knock over a coffee mug full of cigarette ash. Her breathing deep and controlled. Then it was happening. The rope went around and under. Rubbed my skin raw. 'Pan,' she said. 'Stands for panic' pulling a knot tight between my shoulder blades. 'Don't let the bastard win.'

Transpose. Transform. Ovid. Always Ovid.

The Bald-Knob was calm, patient. Focused on the glow of each new organ. As Blue tightened the knots I heard blood humming in my ears, whispering secrets. Jamie's stick whistled past me as she tied on more layers, under armpit, through thigh, pulling my arms and legs behind me and knotting them together as I lay on the floor. The last of the rope she looped around my neck over and over. Softly tightened it. My face swelled beetroot and aubergine, eyes translucent as lychees. I wouldn't give her the safe word. The room was blue and white fireflies.

She was taking the soul from the carcass. I felt it rush through my body, everything I'd been holding, Maw's scream left me. The rope burned her out. I soaked in the white feedback of a guitar leant against its amplifier. The rope burned me alive and I was released. A deer running through thickets, escaping gunfire. The more the rope tightened around my body, the lighter I felt, projected outwards.

She loosened the noose. Otherwise, I wouldn't have stopped her. I was gluttonous. Space collapsed back into me, an explosion in reverse. I gulped over the hooks in my ribs. Stared up at spiders and moths fossilized around a naked light bulb. Everything had a disgusting body, everything. I saw nipples erect through her shirt. She undid each knot and massaged the skin with her palm. Rubbed minty ointment over the burnt parts. I was let loose, limp, humming. She wrapped a blanket around me. We sat side by side and a strange tingling played on my features. The ghost pulling on door handles, finally had a way out.

'How'd you get that?' she said after a while, pointing the li-on's-tail tip of her rope at my face.

'My brother threw a stick into it when I was five,' I said.

'Sibling rivalry?' she said.

'Out of love,' I said, quietly. I needed a drink. We needed a drink. We both knew it. Both felt it deep inside of us. It had been our last meeting after all. I got dressed. Walked to the Deli. Bought whiskey. Bought cigarettes. Fluff in the change. Walked back. Light as a feather. Elated. I poured us two measures. Blue drank it down quickly and coughed. Her sleeve slipped and I saw a scaffolding of scars running down her forearm. She saw me and rolled up the other. They bulged and twisted thickly.

'That's my signature,' she said, twisting her arms around in candlelight.

'Feels familiar,' I said. We sat in silence and I refilled our glasses. I thought of flue fire in wood burners, how the sap of moist wood gets caked up along the piping, flammable, waiting to explode up through the chimney. We drank, lifting our arms like wind-up monkeys, feeling the stone-cold sobriety of our days and months submit to this dragon fire, watching a wild herd descend to trample us.

'Ever heard about the battle of the trees?' she said. I shook my head frustrated that I hadn't. The Bald-Knob had no record of this. Where was he? 'Two alphabets. One was ancient Irish, carved into stones. The other derived from observing the flight patterns of cranes in the sky. I read about them at a time when there wasn't a language for me. I decided to make my own battle of the trees with vodka and a penknife.' She downed another, poured a third. Scars written all the way up into her biceps.

My phone started ringing. Clanging against the whiskey glass. It rang and rang and I looked at it ringing. And there it was again, the thing I couldn't see. One paw in front of the other. A stick in my eye. Blue tossed it onto me. Unknown number. The night swirled. A handful of strange names for groups of animals. Like cattle prods, I held the names out in front. Lodged between me and the world. Some things can't be swallowed. Some things always get stuck in the teeth. I knew before I answered and something rolled over in my stomach. A man's voice said my name. Out of his depth with the message. I knew, I just knew.

A Cowardice of dogs

An Intrigue of cats

A Skulk of foxes

A Cauldron of bats

'Is that Blake, Jamie Ackerman's brother? said the voice.

'Who's this?' I asked.

'Arkansas state police, sir. There's been an accident. We're really very sorry,' it said. The smell of sulfur. The Bald-Knob stopped pruning and looked up. Noises on the line. Microphones in wool.

'Yes?'

'Fire. Arson, we think. I understand you've been gone for a while. We need you down here to collect your brother's remains.' The words started to disintegrate in my ear. I said something and hung up.

Bloom of jellyfish

Exaltation of larks

Shadow of jaguars

Shrewdness of apes

I put the glass down. Resumed my position. Knelt, nodded to the rope. Blue understood. She poured me a new drink. As she tied, Pan sat on my chest, clicking his tongue. 'Soon,' he mouthed. All the cigarettes I had ever smoked fell out of that word. Broken, half-sung odes played in my head smothered in cotton, a few notes here and there poking through the owl's pellet thought. I was on the floor. She tied me until dawn rolled in. The Bald-Knob opened up his broken wing. He threw up bile to protect me.

Me—a child that slept under the wingspan of a carrion bird.

BLUE

When he woke up, she had covered the walls in post-it notes. So that they smothered everything. So that they ate up his living room. Chair legs, books and lampshades devoured by her thoughts. By a language translated from scars, to wolves, to poems. She tried to picture Harmswood from the little material he'd given her. Tried to picture the town that kept coming back to finish him off. The texture of wet earth and his little brother and the faucet dripping. The front door wide open. Stretched on its hinges. Leaning into cotton fields.

Blue had never been around fields or countryside. They were paints on a canvas. She'd been up all night, thinking as he slept on the floor with his back turned. All through her scribbling and pacing, he never woke once.

As the city groaned awake and morning thinned the sky, she walked out into the neighborhood. Down to the corner for coffee and pastries, her mind moved in somersaults. She'd been off the meds for a week and circles widened inside. Boxes and closet doors opened up so that bats filled the tidy little room—the preserved exhibit. They shat all over its perfectly positioned furniture, chattered from the rafters. Her fingers were tingling and raw from the rope as she handled coins, shoulders tight as stone. When she came back inside, Blake clutched at her chest, mouthing something. Two steaming coffees she bought fell to the floor. Blue watched him calmly like a crow picking at the brains of a dead cat. An intelligence, space-time condensed. Car fumes, rotting banana peel, all the rats beneath them planning their attack. It was the booze, the cockroach stupidity of these thoughts. Pan stood in panic. From scars, to wolves, to poems. They both crouched low to feed and light thinned the sky.

CATHARTES-AURA

Immolation is sacrifice by ritual burning. Self-sacrifice. To gods seen and unseen. A god can be anything. A god can be loud like thunder or gentle as feathers on a thermal wind. This is what trauma teaches. This is what wounds teach you. That all gods require offerings. That they lurk. That they all wait in the tall grass. That they watch a person unfold.

BLAKE

The thickness of Vern's thumb. Pressed on the back of my neck. Old fires, how silently they burn. As a boy, cigarettes worked well with ev-erything. Good company. Lighting up with Jamie in middle school. In restrooms and behind water closets. Our bodies bent out the window, split in two as Maw danced and screeched beneath us. Smoking was a way of feeling our weight in space. Breathing ourselves back into the world. My voice didn't get any deeper. Hairs didn't sprout over my chest. Jamie got the hang of it quicker. He lit up the old with the new as I coughed, holding it in too long. His body was built for fire.

    Maybe it wasn't as bad as all that. Kids made things up. Con-fused things. Memory was fickle, you couldn't trust it. It squirmed and stung like snatching a jellyfish out of the water with your bare hands. It was difficult to understand what happened to us back then. In many ways, I never left Harmswood, Arkansas. It may have been an accident—when you are poor, none of it matters. My uncle made us hammer nails into pawpaw saplings so that Maw wouldn't have more accidents like us. He said it was the old family way. The same reason all her men left from the same door they came in from, so as Maw wouldn't get pregnant again. Funny how something becomes normal until you say it out loud. How it is suddenly an entity. The old ways were kept by some before the asphalt was laid down, when all was dirt roads. I remember hammering those nails in with my brother like they were my siblings, other brothers and sisters I'd never meet, never kick up anthills with. I hammered my fingers bloody, so Jamie knocked the nails in for me before Vern saw. We had to get them all stuck in the wood before sundown. My earliest memories after the accident are of trees full of nails and Maw's wet bedsheets spread, hanging from the branches of a pawpaw tree. Corncobs burning in a mound and eggshell tea on the stove. Anything and everything to purge her of her accidents. We drove nails into tree bark, to stop ourselves recurring. We killed ourselves as children.

Some animals are wired to eat their young when danger approaches. Others merely to play with them like a cat does a small bird. Jamie was outside, I was inside—this was our greatest difference. But both of us watched the same world simmer out like coals. They say that for suicidal people, the choice is simple. It's standing on the ledge of a burning building. A choice between jumping off or turning back into the flames. I hadn't talked to him. I didn't know his life. He was more a specter than flesh and blood. But somehow, it was all real, at least as an emotion it was real. I never saw any of our dogs die. Only the carrion left behind. I left Harmswood and it swallowed my entire family. Maw and Vern were the last remnants of old Ozark. The bitumen divided our generations. My brother caught fire. He turned back into the flames. You can't escape that, you can't unsee that.

BLUE

They split. Later that morning. After the crack of dawn. They boarded the Greyhound with one-way tickets and hangovers humming. Strapped in until Little Rock and then a second bus up to the northwest. He should have felt angrier, sadder, weaker, stronger, numb. But it was only an Ozark feeling. Only a cloud of pin-needled sensation. Birds inside people and people inside birds. *Birdies*, he said his mother called them on a good day. *Icky-little-bean-sprouts*, on a worse one. It felt good to leave the dot and line game behind her. All the lovely Maureens with their cracked eggs and nibbling fish. It felt good be moving towards the prospect and vastness of fields.

CATHARTES-AURA

Honk. Hiss. Puke.

BLAKE

The bus was empty. No one cared about the creation state. Just us and an elderly couple, whispering to each other under red baseball caps. They opened Tupperware and ground up pastry with their molars. It was a three-day drive and my phone kept buzzing with unknown callers. I hadn't quit the gallery job.

Outside the city, the road stretched endless, nameless. The ground was the same color as the sky. Street after street rolled away. The sinkhole will get you, the more you kick, the more it'll suck you down. As we were pulling out of the city, I saw the ditch-witch standing on a street corner with her trolley and stray cats looking up at her, clawing at her bags. In the bone-white morning, she was still. Blue slept deeply after our relapse. Her dreams were wombs while mine were windpipes closing. I'd miss the Bald-Knob if he ever left me. I'd feel incomplete. He was the full embodiment, the symbol, the brushstroke. They weren't as snaggle-toothed and grim as they were made out to be through the ages. Rather important, rather misunderstood creatures, rather crucial to the rotation of things. He was a caretaker to me, a recycler. He cleaned me up. A turkey-vulture's Latin genus meant catharsis, purification, purgation—it meant squeezing out the poison. The Bald-Knob scratched himself oblivious. He trusted me like a twin. I was grateful. Grateful for his hunger.

Blue had my back in this and that was enough.

'I'm not insane,' I said to her.

'Yes, you are,' she mumbled.

'Something really bad happened to me and my brother back then. Like evil-bad,' I said and tried to hide. She stared at me, really stared.

'Whatever it is, turn it into a weapon. Own the darkness, wear it like armor,' she said and punched my shoulder. 'Be *of* the night.'

Trees grew large in reverse. Landscape took over. Small roads wove off into the hills and led to places that weren't really there, like my hometown. Country songs filtered in and out through the radio. Twanging guitars. The freeway didn't exist last time I came through, it was all dug up—dark earth piled up on each side. Workers in the shade, exhausted. The wild was cleared out over time by a fat artery. The first time, it seemed more worth it. There was no doubt in my mind that the only way was forward. The journey back now was less luminous.

Rot. That's how it began. Business behemoths like Walmart sunk it all. In the years since I left, it rolled in like an angry hoard, raped and pillaged, kept the spoils and left the villages in ashes behind it. Everyone was twitching in their own skin. Blowing themselves up in meth labs. Each mile gave way to old oil wells, trailer parks and large drills that sat alone and impotent. The further out we drove, wildlife changed. Atmosphere changed. Hawks replaced pigeons, roadkill be-came more interesting. My heart grew bones over the asphalt and the wheels kept turning. An armadillo rocked on its back with each passing vehicle.

BLUE

Humidity crept into her wound. A failed escape from when she landed badly off the second floor of a clinic, dislocating her shoulder with a bubble wrap pop. They'd taken all her notebooks away. Her words weren't the balloon alphabet of hope, dreams, and rainbow-cake icing. They didn't chime well with the efforts of group counselors and ham-armed nurses. They made cheeks flush and double-chins wobble with concern. All she wanted to be at the time was a sharp edge, a tool to bust things open. She whispered into the ears of others, tried to undo the helpful rhetoric spoon-fed to them each day. *Fox in the henhouse syndrome*, she murmured to herself. All Blue wanted to be was her fa-ther's ashes, shaken free by the winter wind. She jumped off that sec-ond floor and was a lousy cat. Now the southern damp made sure she didn't forget just how lousy a cat she was. Her joints moaned and the twang of it jolted her awake.

She had one eye open for the whole ride. Everyone knew or heard enough stories about the crazy carnival of persons drawn to Greyhound journeys. Everyone had heard of random beheadings in the middle of nowhere. She even put keys between her fingers, just in case. Blake wriggled around like he had worms. Her sunglasses hung lopsided on his face. Fingers bitten to the quick. She watched a road-sign decorated with bullet holes fly past and pressed her tongue up into the roof of her mouth. It all caught up to Blake; the less he looked at it, the closer it got. Waiting for him to falter and slip. After the phone call, he realized that it was in his blood all along. That his mother came from the gutter. That he was bred in that gutter, as was his brother. A door had opened up beneath him and there was nothing left to do but fall awake. The ropes were there too, gently coiled by her side. To tie is to liberate. She leant her head back against the glass and let the road rattle her bones for a while.

CATHARTTES-AURA

Puke. Hiss. Honk.

BLAKE

I slept and was thankful for that small grace—that stone's sleep. We were both drinking again. Unashamed this time. We made sure there was at least a six-pack we could scrounge at every pit stop or swap something for a near empty bottle of something brown. But it wasn't central anymore, the drinking. It had moved away to the periphery as Old Luce yawned wider with each passing mile leaving little room for much else. Wilf Batty stood in the corner of every room we slept in. He followed me all the way back home, guided me even. A shadow the size of a small dog. He was with me now; the way he was with my uncle. Back when all the world's children were just accidents.

It took a good few days. We stopped in motels. Filled their ashtrays up to the brim. Slept in the same bed. Attempted sleep, staring into different corners of the room. Headlights pulled in and out over the walls. She was sullen. For most of it, we kept to ourselves and didn't speak much. In the middle of the night, her side of the bed would be empty. Blue was changing and I'd noticed the imbalance. I'd hear water running in the bathroom trying to drown her voice, or her pen and the paper she kept crumpling up in her fists. Moody plateaus and manic peaks. I thought I knew what was happening. I never challenged her on it. Never doubted her judgement for one second. Her mind flexed and curled like the fingers of Ma's hands in the moonlight.

As we got closer, I could see a storm had rolled in. The driver said it was a small tornado. A young buck of a tornado, testing its strength. The land seemed hurt by it. Tree after tree uprooted and splintered. 'I can almost hear them sighing,' whispered Blue. We passed destroyed barns, splintered roofs, roots in the air like insect legs. Some cows still grazed oblivious to the destruction around them. It felt like a transformation, like some hammer had been brought down from above to destroy and rebuild. A creative violence woven into the very rhythms of nature. Blue used to be called Emily. She changed her name before we met. She said it was a way of shedding parts of herself away. Parts that stung. Letting the new grow from the old. She'd never been this far south before, where everything was layered in snakeskin—everything lay under a tapestry of old selves.

The last passengers tapered off long before we reached Harmswood. It was a slow thinning out, each town sparser than the last. The people living there changed, the lightness drawn out of them and I knew we were close. By the time we passed the big lake, we were all on our own. I knew the driver wanted it to be over as much as I did. I could see it in the way he kept shifting in his seat, checking the radio, twisting the knob on the AC. I saw he had photographs stuffed into the sun guard. Lovers, mothers, wives, children. A car he wanted but could never afford. Something to live for on long drives through hinterlands, all those drive-through states. Solitary stretches where time hardened and warped the mind.

I saw it draw into view. Nothing had changed. I already knew it. The bent sign was as I left it, the bus-stop still with its two vertical steel poles missing a bench. The silhouette of the mountain. The moon lit from the bottom. We all lived under the same moon. For some reason I always felt it as a she.

Waiting behind black holes, sinkholes and the animal's mouth yawning. Too much electricity dulls things. Kills the light that's already there. We stepped out onto the hunting ground and the bus made a U-turn. It was the stench that hit us. Putrid. Vile. A million dead cats left to decompose. The problem had gotten so much worse over time. Ignored. The buzzards hadn't come back and the rot spread further and further outwardly. I held a hand to my mouth. Blue walked over to the side of the road, stretched herself wide open. She put her hands on her hips, pushed her pelvis out in front of her, moan-ing out the hours, the days, the motels. It was hard to have a single thought on that ride. Hard to not just keep counting my breath like coins. She dry-heaved as she breathed in.

'I never thought it could be so bright with the lights out. Too bad it fucking smells like death,' she said. wincing.

'You'll see all kinds of lights out here. It's that out-in-the-sticks melancholia. A space that needs to be filled with something,' I said rambling with adrenaline. I looked to the black mass over the way, a deeper shade than darkness. 'We were told that the souls of dead folks got stuck in those pines on their way to heaven.' I watched her rotate her shoulder. Shook her legs out like juice boxes. We had to walk the rest of the way.

'I haven't missed this place,' I said and spat between my feet. My posture changed a little. Spine more curved. Something in the shoulders twisted and moved forward as I sucked my ribcage back in. I slipped into the shape of myself as a boy in a matter of seconds. A rotten breeze made the grass sing. Little feet tottered at the edge of the asphalt. Her hand on my shoulder.

'You haven't missed it because you never went anywhere,' she said. I thought about her ropes on my skin. The comfort of constraint. That magic in burning it all away. That's what they all believed out here. Fire could erase the truth. Hide it from God.

'Where to, country boy?' she said in a choked voice as another wave of stench hit us. The fields must've been full of dead creatures, dead plants, for the smell was as big as the sky. Luckily, the moonlight didn't reveal too much too early. Only the asphalt glimmered. I hadn't thought that far ahead. I hadn't thought about where to start once I came back. There is a thinness that comes with intensity. It coats the world like a balm, keeps you alive. That's the first thing I felt. Through the numbness. The house. We had to start with Vern. The other was still too big, my brother was too alive.

'About twenty minutes that way, I guess,' I said, pointing to a sparse cluster of lights from the trailer park. I was glad Blue couldn't see me as I walked ahead of her. Straight towards the speckled lights. I remembered the howls we pretended not to hear. The howls Maw made us believe we weren't hearing. One time, Jamie took me out of the house when she passed out. We went into the woods. Slowly, like thieves. I wasn't afraid because he wasn't afraid. He told me to scream until my lungs hurt. Told me we had to show them that we weren't afraid.

I pictured him on the asphalt in the years after I left. I thought of what we said we'd never be and how I betrayed that promise. Cra-ters must've formed in his brain. Even if I couldn't face specifics, I knew enough. I knew enough by the dropped tone of his words in each voicemail, the slur of a dropped tongue. I thought of him walking up to the pay phone and digits jumping around as he tried to dial. How many times he must've hung up. I pictured him asleep in the woods, naked and covered in leaves. Saw his purple face and tried not to count the years. They didn't even fit on my fingers anymore.

We walked on. The Bald-Knob was bloated, so full he couldn't eat. Back where he belonged. Here, there was a tale of a giant buzzard called the Bald Knob who only had one good wing and flew in circles for eternity. He felt distant now. After I realized that Wilf Batty had been hiding inside him. That he had tried to eat the child but couldn't digest. Tried to excarnate him, but the soul was stubborn and wouldn't leave. The slow boy had pushed his way through and was here with me now. I suddenly stopped needing the bird. Demoted from the barri-cade of words I used to dissociate. Exiled back to where he was born. Hatched from a blue egg, in a cave, in the fall. He was still there some-where above my body. The road was that space between Prometheus and the buzzard that tortured him.

Growing up, I rarely walked the asphalt—that was for my brother, for his feet, his pain, his sadness. So many years I spent inside focusing on words, pushing the wild away. The wild that lived in the walls of our home and slept beneath the floorboards. Wilf came back as a turkey-vulture. Every time I saw the birds, they were him in some way, the remnants of that boy trying to say my name, over and over. That was the last thing I saw before Jamie blinded me. I saw the carrion bird trying to eat him. Trying to eat the evidence of what goes on in blank spaces on maps. Smoky fall leaves in my nostrils. The men away. Dogs and gunfire in the distance. Us in the woods and that bad feeling all over again, sitting heavy. Jamie's little shoulders and crooked legs. The stillness. That rustling sound a few yards ahead of me. Creak of rope. Creak of weight hanging from a low branch. The boy tied. The feathered fiend nibbling into his side. That moment. In that moment, the two blended as one. Bird and boy. Before I was split by an event horizon. They were an all-animal, a howler, a victim of fate.

Over the way, someone tried to jumpstart a motorbike. Blue rasped through the chill, trying to light a cigarette. I glanced this way and that. Memories fragmented as firebugs. My feet were off the ground and I was floating up to the fishbowl moon. Blue's lighter flicked. Each flick tugged me back down to the ground so that I wouldn't drift away. I wondered if she still had that dream with wolves tearing her limb from limb. I took her hand.

The fields on either side were bare. I could feel them. Naked, nude, exposed. Charred empty lots that smelt thickly of sulphur. It was almost fall. The last few days of August. But the burning seemed premature. The mist got into our eyes and made us nauseous. It slid into our bodies, slowly loosening bolts. Only the moon and the sparse streetlights and wobbling fire in insects guided us. I didn't know what to expect from my uncle. I couldn't picture him anymore. He was only a cloud of sensation. Tobacco smoke, itching and bumpy skin. He was the world gone gooey. He was Old Luce's mouth opening wide and a worrying uncomfortable wetness. A mess. I didn't know if confronta-tion was the answer, if rage was the answer, if forgiveness was even a word anymore. I struggled to catch my breath.

'I got you,' said Blue, her palm pressed on my bony chest. 'I really never left,' I said.

Even with all of this, I hadn't changed. I was still that child. The eager kid that ran to help him when he called. Ran to please. Who rode with him into the woods with everything that needed to disappear. I had to go back to where I planted my eye as a seed all those years ago.

I needed snakes to be snakes and condoms to be condoms. We were closer to the house now. I recognized how the ground started to lift in a curve before we turned off the asphalt to hit the gravel path. I wondered if he still slept in his shack. Blue mumbled behind me. To herself at first. Then a littler louder as she tugged my hand. We stopped walking. Everything changed.

I gasped, swallowed, and stopped. The roof came into view. The front drive, the truck and the wide-open gate. Suddenly everything was not so numb, not so distanced. Not so broken up by internal laughter. The rope that liberated me, constricted like his hands did. Sandpaper hands carrying me to the truck, buckling me up. His hands pulling my brother off screaming each time he found me lying there. His hands on a steering wheel, the skin on his fingers darkened from an ember getting closer and closer. His palm over my heart, pushing me gently down to the ground as I watched another dog sink, another guardian. Rope sang in those hands when everything else stopped singing.

The house was hibernating. Boarded-up windows. Paint all but peeled off from that one summer when Maw wanted something dif-ferent done to the place. The yard overrun with weeds. Ivy cascaded through old machinery. Vern had let everything go to waste. It mim-icked nature. I could feel it. It wouldn't be long now. Wouldn't be long until he, too, was with Maw, back in the cave of their infancy—out somewhere where stars imploded and were reborn. The shack was a little further out. Behind old feeding troughs. I saw he was in there. A small light from under the door shimmered. Too old for his nocturnal drives. I walked towards it. I strode on and there it was—rage. Burst through me like a feral pig wanting to gore and gore and gore and leave him writhing full of holes on the floor. I got there but didn't knock. Breathed, shivered. Puked all over my boots.

BLUE

What would he say to the wolf at the door? When it was no longer an image in his brain. No longer a folktale to caution the kiddiewinks. When it was all flesh and bone and slobbering mouth. How would he stop the child running? How does anyone stop running? It was the ear-ly hours of the morning, before black turned to blue and then to pink. Life was all the things you never noticed, unless you had to. Unless you were made to. The low growl under the surface of everything. He blocked it all out by seeing faces in the trees, in the leaves. By thinking he could make black cats burst into flame by flipping them the bird.

He told her that birdsong dissolved into white noise as they said his brother's name over the phone. As they told him the impossible had happened. A godly thing. An ungodly thing. Blue saw it was real, real pain now. They said the words but he hadn't heard them. In her mind's eye, Blue sketched Pan on Blake's chest once more. He crushed the last breath from his lungs with his swollen blue balls and pressed a finger to his lips. Blake's brother had chosen fury. He'd chosen to make use of the ashes. Blue pictured her father face down in the snow. The swell in a streetlight flickering so that his body was both there and not there, over and over again. Never fully present—cut to black.

BLAKE

You will remember this. This was not a bird in my head. Or a dead boy. Or my brother—another dead boy. This was not therapy. I stood there and my stomach was drowning kittens. Fists pressed into my thighs. I wouldn't budge and the rage began to wither. He'd be old now. A sack of potatoes. Afraid of his own shadow. Of me, when I got too tall for him, too sinewy. I could snap him in two if I wanted. I could shatter him like glass. I thought these things but they weren't real, not at the heart of it. There was me as a child, in the fall as God turned his back on us. A taste of soil and webbed velvety tendrils, a membrane over the tongue and the world rippling, dribbling, each thought a small wave. My body in that soil. In that mouth, yawning. *You will remember.*

Feet shuffled behind th e shack's door. Shuffling—that soun d meant I was outside of myself. Floating up to the moon. I put myself into a moth. Always into a creature with wings. Pulled and unmoving. Stuck between burning fields and wilderness. What do you say to the wolf at the door? Flick/Flick/Flick. Blue walked up, pushed me aside, stepped over the pool of drying bile and pummeled the door with both her hands. She beat it hard and screamed out for him to open. She wasn't scared. She hammered the daylights out of that rotten door.

'Let me be,' said a small voice. 'I'll blow your fucking guts out.' I put my hand on her shoulder and stepped forward. Just in case the wolf still had his teeth. He would take me first. In the olden days, the accused were tied to a post and slowly devoured by mad, ravished animals. In our family, all of us were being slowly eaten by a mad sick thing whose hunger reached up to the sun and clamped it in its jaws. We were all chased. We were all haunted. Grass rustled on the rim of our minds and fingers tapped the glass.

'It's Blake, sir,' I said. My Ozark twang slithered out from where it had been coiled all those years in the city. I turned to Blue. Turned for the eyes of a human looking back. For a commander to push me over the trench.

She nodded. 'Own this,' she mouthed.

'I said it's Blake. Open up now.' My heart. Where was it? Some-thing creaked. Something cracked. Footsteps. The light bloated with his body. The house loomed to my left. I hadn't yet dared to glance. I knew Vern still wouldn't be sleeping there; he was just as superstitious as I was. I felt him standing on the other side. Felt his tall lanky weight lingering. The heavy skull and protruding brow. The deep-set eyes. A horse's neck muscles. He unlocked the door. Stood still for a moment. He'd aged badly, all caved in and his beard yellow. His fingernails over-grown as he fingered a cigarette out of a pack of Marlboros Reds. The left hand shook uncontrollably.

'We're all a little long in the tooth for family reunions, don't you think, boy?' he said and pushed the door open a little wider.

The reek was harsh. It hit us in the back of the throat. Blue gagged but I knew it well. The unwashed. It was the same smell as a city's subway. The smell of people with a head full of demons, spitting at the ground, screaming at the sky. That same urine smell. We cupped hands over our noses. Everything soaked in purple light from dying embers in a wood burner. I'd never been inside his shack before. It was forbidden. My eye adjusted to the darkness and Blue nudged my ribs. Piles of women's clothes were on the dirty floor. Bras and panties. Skirts. Wigs, heart-shaped trinkets. The window was covered up in gar-bage bags. Vern sat down in small wooden chair. Cradled his shaking hand.

'You ever think about your blood, boy? How we've been drop-ping like flies down here? How the rot's turned the bread black? You ever spare a thought for your poor Ma? I told you she'd kick it if you left. Had to burn her up in the end. Didn't want the worms getting in her,' he said. I tried to fight the child that obeyed, that sank, that whis-pered back answers and followed him around with eyes fixed to the ground. I tried. The ditch-witch still stood on the street, in the corner of my memory. My mother. My brother's mother. Just accidents. Nails in tree trunks. A little red stain on the bedsheet.

'Hoped you might've gone with her,' I muttered so he didn't hear. He leaned in more animated. Spoke to me like he used to, like I was sitting next to him in a pickup. Letting me in on a cheeky secret. As if he needed my help with something very important.

'They've had my goats, you know. Every last one of them, tak-en in the night. They don't even eat them. Just mess with the carcasses. Leave them splayed out and slutty for old Vern to find in the morning. Old Vern will clear it. He'll make it all go away,' he said and clutched his shaking hand. Clutched it tight. Even his limbs wanted freedom.

I grew cold. Hearing the high lyrical voice coming out of this large man. Talking as if in a trance. The wood popped in the stove. Blue stood firm. She was the last structure standing in a city bombed to the ground. Liberty among ruins. Vern breathed like his lungs had collapsed. He wouldn't look at me, only through me. Only at Blue as she walked up to him. My palms were wet. She crouched down to his eye-level. My uncle frowned. The cobra that came out during deer sea-son was merely snakeskin draped over an armchair.

'You a man?' he said, nodding at her. One eyeball veered off to the left, bloodshot. All his features twisted, gnarled, overgrown. A hint of lipstick coated his lips. Some female outfits were on coat hang-ers. Suits of armor, waiting to be worn for battles in the dark, on all those nights when we heard the tires squeal like beat dogs. All those mornings when we were told not to speak to him, to treat him tenderly. When he was grey and the boy-shadow followed at his heels.

'I am this,' she answered calmly.

'No, you're a boy,' he said. 'That's a boy's body,' One of the strings in his voice broke. His chin dropped to his chest. 'I know a boy when I see one,' he said softly to himself. A row of beer bottles glinted in the corner with their tops screwed off, filled to the brim with his urine. This was a jail cell, self-imposed exile, a tower of silence. Alone and with no umbilical link. Alone with the woman who kept him com-pany. The person he could never be. War killed even the survivors. It set them free to run as fast as their legs would carry them. Gave them a head start is all. Before it unleashed the hungriest, fastest pack of hounds to hunt them down. No one stood a fighting chance with those odds. He, too, festered with the buzzards all gone.

Old folk said that you buried the limbs of amputees after death so that the dead could come back and find them, so that they wouldn't wander eternally. So that they could be whole once more. I had so much that was amputated, so much that was buried. My limb was my brother, not my eye and not what Vern had taken away. It was Jamie and I still couldn't think of him. I still couldn't articulate that thought, not here, not yet. Immolation, they had said. Burnt offering, they had said. Blue put down her bag and pulled out her three sets of rope. Three is God's number. Three is the number of spheres in the night sky. She set them down at Vern's feet.

'The cops called. Said something bad went down here. Some disaster. I came back to see it for myself,' I said.

'Your little dope-fiend brother burnt the place down is what happened. Exploded like a damn propane tank. He ran all over, on fire. Burnt up the trailers, burnt up the school, the corn, the cotton, the rye. He got all the way to the pines. It don't matter. I'm glad he's gone. Glad he burnt this shit heap to the ground. At least one of you didn't lay down and take it. At least he died fighting,' he said, gulped and shuddered. A strange noise that came from somewhere deep. Hoarse, guttural, a kind of whimper. He stared at the ropes. All anything had ever been to him was an object and Blue cleared her throat.

'Do you remember what you did to your nephew in those woods?' she said. Through the pines, a solar wind. Vern kept wheezing. Like his heifers, confused, awaiting annihilation. It was hard to be kind to him, I knew that. It was hard and yet I couldn't be cruel. I'd wanted to pin him against the wall, press my thumbs into his windpipe until the eyes bulged. I wanted to hear him beg as I towered over him, stronger, more man than he ever was. But none of it happened that way. I stood still, rooted to the spot. He had a hold over me. Even now as an old pile of women's clothes, a piss-stinking wretch; his words still rang true.

'All I recall's heat and mud and men in pieces. I recall being told to take ears and noses. I recall them not caring about us and killing being part of living. It was always a part of living. I recall them, out there, they never went nowhere. They were sleeping, in the mountains getting strong and they demand their pound of flesh. Eye for an eye. Being over there was one war, this one here never ends. They never end,' he said pointing to the spot on his body from where that whimper came. Blue was crouched low staring up at my uncle's features. Alcoholism, mild strokes, or maybe it was just him. His true self, a glitch. A chord built of wrong notes. He looked at her squarely, surrounded by all the naked men and boys he'd never touch, he'd never break. That sound again. That dying thing. Wheezing like the prisoner that lived in the pipes and drains of our house. That sound made me flee Harmswood.

'I never did nothing,' he said slurring. 'That little shit-bag. His name's all he has. Now he goes and drags it through the mud. It's men like me that keep the peace. Me, me, me,' he shouted, thumping out the last three words with his foot. 'I won't have it smeared, your hear?' But he wasn't heard. I moved in closer. Needed to look at him. To see his mind scraped empty. Scratches of broken fingernails down the walls of his skull. I saw him as a boy cowering under a rotten log while the unthinkable was done to his sister. I saw the spindly adolescent crawling around the house, foraging through her make-up bag, painting his face, quivering with a freedom he could only find in the hour of the wolf. I saw him get caught by Maw as she hobbled with a cracked pelvis in insomnia's purgatory. Saw them hold each other in a look of blood-oaths. I felt his man's heart burst as he went through the years carved out of the wrong kind of wood. The map of a body was the only language he could trust. To govern that body was to be a type of strong-alligator-man. As kids we got caught in the crossfire, when his lust was caged and rabid. Caught in the teeth of a sick town and a sick man, as he was. I pitied him. But pity is never forgiveness.

I'd once loved him. More than I dared to admit. Year after year, with my fingers hooked to his belt. Thinking I was safe, thinking nothing bad could happen with him watching over me, guiding me. I traced the flaky bald patches on his scalp. The chipped nail polish, glitter spilled over an empty whiskey bottle. He whimpered. In my shadow now. An object I could finally see. I realized then that he'd always lost.

'Let's go for a drive. Like we used to. I want to show you something,' I said. A tear brimmed. 'I want to tie you up.' Vern pursed his lips. 'We're going to choke the poison out of you,' that's when my voice broke. That's when he looked at me. The soldier. The hidden man who had known death as a set of rosary beads, each one slipping through his fingers into nothing. It startled me; a tear dripped.

'I never harmed the Batty boy. Wasn't me who dressed him out that way,' he said to someone standing outside the frame of the moment. I could see Blue's courage given over to the vast unknown of backwoods, of hill-folk, of tribes and strange animals, to a forest that had a mind and moved in and around everything like a fleet of spies. She didn't understand the language now, that the air down in the Ozarks made the brain buck and snort like an unbroken colt. This was my homeland. Vern continued.

'That I could not do. Hell, they always demand their pound of flesh, son. They'll get it one way or another. It's the balance we've struck. I brought them both back but they were taken anyhow,' he said. 'He wasn't fit for life and so he was theirs. So was Jamie. Both fated,' he said. 'I blame the powder. That foreign powder did this to us. That was the day nature stopped. I blame the black stuff in the rye that turned your Maw stupid. I blame the government for lying to us about it all. I blame God for pissing on us and the Devil for keeping us alive. I blame Nam. I blame you. Only ones I don't blame is them. They were here before and they'll be here after. No matter what you burn away, some roots run too deep. Some of us understand.' He lowered his head, lit another cigarette. 'God backwards is dog,' he said in a singsong, blowing on the ember to even out the burn.

BLUE

The poem sat with her. Fluttered back in from a far-away place. She had stumbled across it in the early days of trying to write. Of compar-ing herself to a million others and feeling at once belittled and amplified by the sheer strength of voices. The lines of this poem were but some of many that had burrowed down deep. But as she stood in the old man's shack with her new friend, her new tying bunny, another soul in recovery. As she juggled the scraps of information Blake had given her, his reaction to the phone call and the power of the rope on his skin, the ropes were always key to unlocking – the ropes turned into the lines of that poem as she stood there observing two very different men. Two colliding spheres of masculinity. It gave her a strength to be there witnessing this. In a dark, damp corner of the universe. It felt archaic. Dream of the earth. Myth of the individual. Somehow it was right that she was there with him at that moment. Blake's childhood felt very loud inside her.

"*The eye satisfied to be blind in fire.*
Over the cage floor, horizons come" –

It was by Ted Hughes. Another man of many deaths, with his ultimate big-cat-poem of childhood. Blue chose those two lines now. Rock hard candy. Indestructible. Filling her with movement. She had to be strong for her tying bunny. For the abused one-eyed boy who had trusted her with his body. She saw that he was still lost and tangled in the brambles. Cut up by the thorns and sharp branches. Still voiceless as the turkey-vultures. The uncle that broke him, that cast such a wide shadow, was only a man to her. Man-shaped trauma. Utterly diagnosable.

She stood next to Blake, telepathically whispering those two lines.

"*The eye satisfied to be blind in fire.*
Over the cage floor, horizons come…"

BLAKE

Maw was always so scared, obsessed with the trees beyond the chicken wire. They owned her heart. She stared at them for hours even when it started raining. Especially in the fall. Even when the wind blew strong and I could see her skin quiver. I wondered where Jamie went in the night. Where he came back from all soiled and raw. I still wondered about that. He wasn't Vern's plaything like I was. Something else had him in its jaws when my back was turned. The old ways had a hold on us all. More and more so as the crops turned black. We believed the cracked nonsense of people left to rot unpurged. We believed in any-thing to justify an atrocity

I walked Vern out of the shack. He didn't resist. The upper arm had grown soft, pillowy. Thoughts of slaughter rose in my mind. He reminded me of one of those old mutts we used to care for. The ones that knew they were being put down. Their cycle closing. I wanted to give my uncle something he would never have felt otherwise. To make him an offering. I wanted to reinvent pain. Through the rub and the burn. I still wasn't real to him. It couldn't be real that this toy, this little rag-doll had come back to life in the dark. There was just about enough gas in the pickup. Blue drove, she seemed confident, upright as Vern sat between us. He stank. He stared blankly at the asphalt shimmeringunder the moon and through a windscreen splattered with insects. I twisted the rope inside the backpack. I had to do it right.

The AC moaned and Vern nudged it with his knees. Over and over until the sound evened out. He knew where we were heading to. He knew the spot. Where we'd been together many times. Many times with bundles in the backseat. Back to the great big mouth. So many times, it meant nothing to him.

We drove past the gas station, black-ened and emptied by the fire. Torn down, all the old pumps fumed. The water tower came into view and I told Blue where to turn off. We wound through flatland and up into the mountain trail. In daylight we'd see the rolling waves of Ozark wilderness. The patchwork colors of fall. We'd see the ravines where water flowed and folk dumped dish-washers. Wooden bridges connected strips of land to each other. We'd cross the lake where I'd fished with him as a boy. The eel-bite scar that whitened with each passing year. There was beauty in this land. Beauty with its people gone forever. I started feeling emotional, instead of list-ing groups of critters; I put straight questions to myself and the answer was always the same:

Did he ever think about me after I left? – No I was meat.

Did he ever miss me? – No I was meat.

Was the fact that I ran away, painful to him? – No I was meat.

I always just dead meat, walking.

BLUE

She drove and thought about tying. Only tying. How the first time it was done to her was the best high. The only significant high after writing something she liked. No person's touch was as good as the rope. No accolades or gifts or sweet words from important people compared. That is what the absence of a mother does to a person, the absence of cradle and breast. It made her shun the human touch and yearn for the constriction and pressure of an object. As she was made object - it filled her body with feathers and then set them all on fire. Until she felt she was breathing this fire. Until all there was was an outward spiraling burn. Nothing in the world was larger than her in that moment, all was spiral. She knew she needed to conjure this for others. To turn people willfully into objects and burn them up as effigies of their old tortured selves. An endless melancholia in the lack of mother.

She turned where he told her to and the uneven earth shook the vehicle. Root and stone. This had to be an ending. It had to draw a line through a word long unspoken. In her head she began to recite the steps to tying a person. One at a time until Blake told her to pull over. One at a time. She knew exactly what to do.

The Shibari Box-tie:

Reverse tension. Start with the middle of the rope. Pass it beneath the breasts. Again, reverse tension. Do an overhand knot to make sure the rope is more secure. Now over. Over again and again. Twist. That's it. Over the shoulder now.

Top to bottom.

Then underneath.

CATHARTES-AURA

Towers of Silence are platforms upon which people place the dead to be picked clean by carrion birds. They believe that the soul is carved out and taken elsewhere. That all gods reside within the human breast. Prometheus is a sky burial bred in the bone of mankind. He will be picked clean even-tually.

BLAKE

The pickup wobbled over the forest floor and pushed into the low branches of an oak tree. We stopped. Got out. The rest was on foot. The world swirled like it had when I was a boy. Vern did not talk. A true P.O.W. The same moisture filled my lungs as it had back then. I couldn't see the mushrooms, but they were there, under us, around us, the charred membranes, crisp and sour prying open the mind's eye and forcing the next world in through my wound. They grew so easily in the Ozarks, fertilized by all the secrets. The spores had been in the air over my town for generations. They had been there before settlements and frontiers. When the English, Irish, and Scots brought their magic with them, it was eaten up by those spores. When they breathed in the forest air, a lotus opened up inside them, a second self. This was our blood, our legacy, our lie. Everything and nothing. I led Blue through the undergrowth memorized, memorial-ized, immortalized in my unconscious. Preserved by the gluttony of a turkey-vulture. The further in we went, trees diversified. They mixed with the ashes and conifers. For every step I fought the chained-up child. I pushed him back against the rock. For the first time in that place of nightmares, that hollow room, I could be separate from him. I could use the rope against itself. The tips of trees still smoked up into the moonlight. Raw bodies pulled stiff from a pyre. Fire was the great equalizer. Fire was love, love of a friend. I had a shield this time, an amazon, a warrior-poet.

We took him to the *Omphalos*. The point at which the world began to disappear. His centre. His nest. The sinkhole was much wider than I'd remembered it, more earth had collapsed, more land shifted as catacombs of forgotten mine shafts gave way. There in a near-perfect sphere where nothing else grew. Where people took what they wanted gone from the world. Every family had its secrets. Here, they offered them all up to Old Luce.

'Kneel down now,' I said to Vern. He shuffled forward. The faded make-up, the leaking mascara, the warpaint made him fierce. He knelt into a large pool of mud and the sky turned lighter with dawn breaking. He knelt grimly, centering his weight. He managed to lift his upper body so that he resembled his former self—tall, lean, weathered. The shaking hand was hidden behind his back. I had to remember the work I'd done. I had to remember Wilf Batty. The loggerhead was bigger, so much bigger. My whole life was tied to his death. This was as much for him as anything to do with what happened to me. It was for all us accidents. Jamie too. All because of a hillbilly superstition. A cracked mysticism. A baseless fabrication that caused so much pain. Hysteria, fear, panic. Vern smiled and shrugged.

'Do what you want, Blake. You're an Ackerman. You seen it all,' he said and flicked his tongue. None of the fumbling and the stum-bling. None of the weakness. It shook me. I was annoyed that it shook me. The world was faces, sneering, smiling, snarling. It was shrieking black cats.

As we stared as each other, I blamed God for the way he turned out. I blamed God for making him think he was an abomination. God in the shape of his father. In the shape of a fist, a belt, a gun. God, the cattle brander. The string of saliva. The hole where vocal cords should be singing. Born with a boot on his neck. My grandaddy's sickness swam through the blood, through the canals, the cave systems of our ancestral consciousness. That creature looked in from behind our eyes.

'I want to show you a good thing. Just once.' I said in a whisper. Softly. Not to trick. Not to mock. But to somehow melt the boundary between us. Through the psychotropic curtain of my childhood. The smells and senses. That old weight in the gut. Vern lowered his head back down.

Feeling sorry is a type of understanding. We stood there in the forest, city people, with our Japanese ropes. We stared at him. The Vietnam survivor. The cattle farmer's son. The twin that buried his other half. The man full of fury with unquenched desires. He was the embodiment of it, the reason for picking up and running. The reason for drinking myself into oblivion. The reason Jamie was ash and dust now. It was my guilt for realizing I hadn't ever truly forgiven him for blinding me, not with my whole heart. Vern was the ropes binding me to the rock of my past, a past I pushed against with the violence of every addict. Cathartes-Aura, mine was the only turkey vulture immune to the color turquoise.

Now was the chance to transform. To transpose into weird new light. A warm glow for the young. It was a choice to go back in deer season. The fall when men hunted the gods.

I took the ropes and began tying up my abuser, my whisky-barreled alligator man. I recited it all in my head. Tied him as Blue had tied me. In the hope that he would feel the same removal. He was limp. Loose as a goose. No resistance. Out there under the pines, he was quiet. It stunk of burnt timber and the spores of fungus got up our noses. Blue whispered instructions when I got a knot wrong, calm, always calm. Ankles to wrists. A harness and I hogtied my uncle. Next to the sinkhole. Under a bone-white sky.

Hours, light-years. Blue secured the final ties on Vern, fastened him. The old man chirped like a small bird beneath the rope. Whim-pered beneath my book-soft palms. I felt the same intensity of when Ja-mie and I plucked little chicks from under their mother's from between their strong talons. We cupped the handfuls of warm fuzz next to our faces. Trying to push heart into head and make us merge. I stood back. When I raised my head, I saw a shape in the trees. A white porcelain torso up above. I saw the body of Christ in a pine tree. Fake droplets of blood at his temples. Eyeballs turned up, fixed away from us.

I drifted over to the god in the trees. The hunted god. The lurking god, who sacrificed himself, to himself. They were all the same. Scattered pieces of a broken heart. Someone had wanted Christ swal-lowed up by Old Luce. Someone wanted her to make him disappear. Instead, he was thrown into the branches, caught in the teeth, meat too tough to swallow. A tough church ornament. I don't know how long I stared up at him. This creature. Something was happening. Something warm. The Bald-Knob was a black dot over the mountains. Perched in the caves where his kin used to roost. I didn't need him. The rope was my undoing. I looked at Jesus the amputee, the half-man, the doll. I looked at Jesus, the loon, the man who slept in the pines. Only his crown of thorns looked real. Something shifted in the corner of my eye.

A large stag. A whitetail buck. Thick-necked with a crown of thorns all his own. He stared me down. This king stomped a hoof. Ducked his upturned saber-toothed head and snorted beneath the pale torso. Blue didn't see him. Only I did. He'd come for the ritual. The womb-fantasy. The christening. I turned to look at my bound uncle. Bound and happy in surrender. Hog-tied like the loggerhead child. He was smiling. Eyes screwed shut in bliss. Blue kept checking the knots like a mechanic. Tenderly making sure he was secure. Tears came. Real tears. When I looked back, the buck was gone. Gone into the morning before the guns and the dogs came. Only Christ the half-digested re-mained, straining to see the sky for the trees.

BLUE

There was silence in the world after that. She took a moment to listen for it in the sounds of the forest, for leaves crackling in laughter and for the foreign birds conversing. But there was only an aftermath. Stunned in the wake of it all. There was only herself; poised like Gretel in the middle of deep dark woods. A million folktales born and reborn out of the movements between trees. For a moment that's all there was and she liked it. She liked and appreciated her role within those hidden machinations. She was exactly where she was supposed to be.

They left the old man where he was and nature would somehow take its course. For he was never allowed to be a person. He could only be mythical. A thing awkwardly composed of other things. Heads, legs, tails, wings—wound up into a body and told to exist that way for a lifetime. Who could bear the sight of themselves in that light? Who could bear the weight of their own flightless wings? Blue knew that very bad things had happened where she now stood. Without being given specifics. She could feel it rising up to grab her legs from the soil. Things that destroy a person and fill them to the brim with monsters. Blue didn't need much else. It felt like good work. Not hateful. Not vengeful. But pure. A purge. It was the best thing one could do for a fiend like Blake's uncle. For one of those beasts in fairytales. One of those movements between trees. For someone who abuses the child in themselves through turning other children into objects of abuse.

She kept her palm between Blake's shoulder blades, softly pushing him away and out of the pinewood. The sky was rinsed out like a rag. A curtain of starlings. A curtain of heartbeats swelled and collapsed across it.

CATHARTES AURA

Odin has two ravens that fly over the world. One of them is thought. The other is memory.

Two sides of the same mind.

They caw to make the world listen.

BLAKE

Jamie simply caught fire. After a beating that cracked his eye sockets. After days in the hole. After this man questioned him about a missing girl. The one mangled by our dog years back. I knew what they were trying for. They needed someone to jail. My brother was a nobody who wore the wrong t-shirts, who listened to the wrong music, who had problems no one in the world cared about. They'd stuck him in a chair, starved and concussed, trying to force a confession. Trying to plant the seeds of memory and make him dream up blood on his hands. They told me he combusted right there in that chair while the camera rolled. He'd finally had enough.

They said he was laughing as he ran, wailing. The walls caught fire, the floor. He kept going down the asphalt. He let out a howl. A howl that will stay in the stones and the sky and the soil. The dryer timber caught light. The fire swung from one tree to the next like an ape. Red clouds over blackened teeth. It was unstoppable they said, devilish. Before they brought him in, they found Jamie curled up in Ma's empty grave asleep. Maybe he lifted the curse, maybe now something clean would sprout from the ashen topsoil. A cleansing. A sacrifice. A new origin. A creation myth for the creation-state.

We drove back to town. The two of us. Left Vern there. The last offering. Jamie had tried purge the land of its vermin. That's all we knew. I could almost hear my brother thinking this as a detective tried to walk me through what happened. One chance in a million. Some-thing that never occurs. They had a shoebox with his charred bones. What they scraped from the patch of earth where he fell. Crammed him in there. Chicken bones. Blue took the box and I shook the detec-tive's hand. When they told me what happened, I was surprised that the trees in the Ozarks were so flammable. Half the mountain burned down, all the way to the fields.

***

I needed to go through the house once before we climbed back on the Greyhound. I would never be back. The knots were all tied. The cops drove us back through town. Houses with large gaps between them. A liquor store with bottles you could count on your fingers and toes. Nothing. The country was cutting Harmswood out of the map. The sleeping dragons were all extinct. The library stood there. A ceno-taph. I squinted to see Mrs. Batty in the window but the blinds were all shut.

Blue didn't really talk since we tied Vern. Since she saw him exhale himself out into the world as the rope tightened. Seeing Vern in that light was a blessing, under the gaze of two lonely gods. The shoebox full of bones was warm in my lap. This may have just been my fantasy of how fire lingered on after being put out. They picked him up piece by piece. Holding him now was like burying a pet out of love. An animal with a name. A pharaoh, a witch, a tyrannosaurus. I was not afraid. Only melancholy. Carl Batty planted the seed all those years back. I saw everything they couldn't see. My brother and I were Viking. My eye and his legs were fated. It was the only way to make sense of what happened. He was heart before head. Born inside the mouth of a great wolf. He was a bold accident. It never mattered to me where he came from. He listened to my stories dragging a stick through the earth, whipping it against trees. We didn't end in a shit town. Our blood sang as all rivers do. Only now, with this small ossuary in my hands, were we reunited. Through untuned guitars and spidery voices. Through a telephone receiver. Through the howl in a seashell.

In daylight, the land was normalized. Still scarred, charred, and blackened by decades of decay. Yet under the sun's gaze it was still only earth and weathered crops and men that didn't look like killers. A run-down rural town full of blind spots and sinkholes. In the daylight, the place lost its bulk and contour. Every speck of rust was visible. Every wrinkle. It sucked the scary out like poison. But you had to survive the night to get there. To see things as they truly were you had to surface through the murk. This was more than just a personal scar. It was the signature of a place gone rotten. Left unchecked. Who'd have thought that killing off a few ugly birds, a few hateful buzzards, could end a country and its people. I thought about these things as on the drive back to the house.

Part of me had always known I'd never see Jamie alive again. I once caught a news story of a bunch of kids up in Salem. A gang of crusty teenagers had infested a house in a middle-class suburb with drugs, sex, and satanism. They changed their names to those of de-mon-princes and spray-painted red pentagrams of the front porch. I saw mugshots of their leader. He had a tattooed face and grimy dread-locks, threaded through with multicolored string. His eyes bloodshot and besmirched with eyeliner. He photographed well. They found two bodies buried in his backyard and arrested him and two of his girl-friends. I imagine they were the ones that threaded some color into his matted hair. He later died in a jail cell. Filed his teeth down to a point and bit his wrists open on a full moon. My skin crawled as I watched the news report. With an inch more privilege. The sheer luck of being born in a different context and a couple more friends. That kid could've easily been my brother; in some sense, Jamie was that boy. Or one of the kids that followed him. He was any boy at a loose end with inherit-ed monstrosities. None of it was his fault. His nor Wilf Batty's.

There was a key to the house, left in the shack. The image of Maw sat rocking in the corner of my eye. One of her nine heads glared. I ignored it, this last phantom. I wondered what to do with it all. Vern's shack, the house, the useless plot of land. An old key with rust on the handle. You had to push it in hard. Slam with the bottom of your fist for the bolts to give. It hurt my palm as I pushed it in, pink and white blotches took shape.

'I'd like to see my room. Then we can go,' I said to Blue as she hung back clutching my brother's box of bones to her stomach. I was sure there was some myth, some lore attached to that moment. A loved one keeping the remains of another loved one. For the life of me, I couldn't place it. My mind was wiped clean, featherlight.

As I pulled the door open, some of me flew out. That little man in the drainpipes ran naked after that hulking black shape into the cotton field. He threw his arms up high into the breeze and croaked. Testing out his vocal cords for the first time, transforming, merging himself. It was Ovid, scrambling and free. I'd finally found him. Finally freed him.

All the rooms were mummified in cobwebs and decorated with mouse droppings. Glints of silverfish darting everywhere. I felt bad that Blue was there. More than everything else, showing her the house, my insides, was most shameful. I knew she could feel the weight of it all pressing down like a paw. I saw the spot at the top of the stairs, where Maw and I sat before the men came to see her. Where I waited for her to pretend to cut me into small pieces that made the skin tin-gle. Tingling, pressure, temperature. Years with a bandaged head and her voice in my ear. Men. Many fathers. Many strangers. Deep voices through the wall. All there, enmeshed in the sarcophagus of home. My mother's crime was allowing it. Allowing all of it.

'Do you see that?' Blue said quietly, pointing through the doorway and out into the fields. She clutched Jamie's bones closer to her chest. Swallowed hard. I saw something run across the road. A shape with limbs galloped. We saw it stop and look at us. Strong and hunched. We watched it pick off fleas at its hip with leathery fingers, snort and grunt. We saw ourselves in its eyes. A breeze made the grass rustle. Blue shivered as a gust brought the stench of it over to us,. I sat down on the top step. Rubbed my hands together. Placed a fiery palm over my good eye. Exhaled.

After the accident, Jamie and I slept through six long days. We didn't eat. We didn't leave the bedroom. He wasn't a wild cat, he wasn't a monkey. The back door slammed. Vern rolled a tin barrel out into the yard. The engine on his pickup growled as he pulled out of the driveway for the final time that night. He'd been coming and going, bringing back heaps of newspapers tied with string. Boxes bundled under his arms. She wanted the town's memory wiped clean.

That night, my brother wasn't sleeping. He just lay there. I felt his body turn this way and that, not knowing where to put himself. The creak of his mattress filled my head. Its springs measured time in spirals. My eye hummed, bristled, and whined. I felt sorry for its loneliness. The last flash of color I saw as the stick entered my socket was a shard of peacock's tail, bright colors streaked and dotted. The tail fanned out inside my dead eye so hundreds of new eyes blinked back. The hanging boy being devoured by a bird.

Maw ran back and forth, trying to find something that wasn't there. Her presence shook the plywood. Manic, they would call it later, when it was too late. I heard her rustling something like leaves in the garden, emptying them into the barrel. Then the back door slammed shut. Her feet on the stairs. Our hearts catching the rhythm of her as she climbed towards us. Sometimes feet on the stairs meant other things. Sometimes men lost themselves in the hallway and Maw had to soothe and smooth their hands away from our faces. She had to guide them back, like a siren to lost sailors. Jamie hadn't said a word in those six days. Not even a murmur.

She slowed down as her feet drew closer to the door. Clawed out. Gathered in my chest as she burst into the room. Breathless. Her nightgown smelled of fire. She stared at us huddled together and then tore the curtains wide open. Beams of light bled in over the walls like we were in a cave. Her hands all over our bodies. Fingers in our hair. Pulling on our cheeks and earlobes. All over Jamie, shaking him awake. Breathless and fire-breathing. She pulled my brother down by the elbow and sat us next to each other on the floor holding our jaws in her charcoal hands. She looked at my face, at the bandages that needed changing. Her lips quivered. I saw her throat move and swallow some difficult mass.

'If we never say it, it never happened, my birdies,' she said nod-ding her head. 'If we didn't see it, it wasn't there. If we didn't hear it, there was nothing there to be heard. Isn't that right my beansprouts?' I could feel Jamie next to me, starting to rock. Back and forth. A difficult mass. I so wanted Maw to stay happy. With all my heart I wanted it. So, I answered for both of us.

'Nothing, Mama,' I said and placed a hand over my good eye. She pulled me into her breast. It felt half-empty and smelt of moth-balls. They filled my head. She reached and pulled Jamie in after me. He was limp and heavy. She whispered spells into our bodies as smoke met the sky. Gibberish that swarmed over our eardrums. I touched my brother's hand and found him cold as stone. At the time, I couldn't understand his resilience to this warmth, this love, this witchcraft of hers. At the time, he annoyed me.

'Let me show you how we kill a thing,' she said, as she tugged at our arms and marched us out into the yard. I loved when Maw talk-ed this way. Food for the young. We got outside and Jamie's skin was kind of blue. The smell in the air was thick, polluted, cooked somehow. Maw took us close to the bonfire and told us to stare into it. Stare until we saw the past go white.

That was the night Wilf Batty burned up in a tin barrel with all the newspapers. She emptied lighter fluid over him and we watched the smoke slither up into the pines. Vern was over by the fence with his back to us. I took Jamie's arm and pulled him around the flames, the heat pushed on our cheeks and eyelids. I pushed and pulled him around until we were dancing like little goblins. We held onto each oth-er and twirled around until the dimming world was a fat brushstroke. Jamie started yelping, hoarse at first from days of silence. I chased him around the burning center, grabbing at his bent legs, pinching his an-kles. Together our voices were the fire. Around and around we went, even though it was cold in the fall. Even though we were in our un-derwear. This is how we survived it, through that burning center in the middle of everything.

Maw laughed. A fist pressed to her moving mouth. She stopped piling on the kindling. Part of me was always watching her. One hand on her hipbone. She stared for a while until her cat's pupil dilated. Ja-mie became loud, his face a crimson ball. It was him that was guiding the dance. He raged. In a flurry, she ran up to us with a large dirty blanket and we all fell on the wet grass giggling. Her fingers dug into our ribs and pinched at our little butt-cheeks as she tried to tickle the pain out. We wriggled around inside that moment with Maw, inside that chrysalis. The bags under her eyes were wet as bruises. She tickled us deep until the memory of Wilf Batty wriggled away and we lay back on the itchy dank blanket, cuddling into her sides.

'Never stop being my birdies,' she said between mouthfuls of belly, blowing raspberries. 'Never fly away.' We screamed with tears streaming down our faces and the glow of that burning boy warmed us. She'd never been so tender with my brother, like she was saying goodbye. We were in the stomach of a whale, in between the soft pinky folds. My eye stung but it didn't matter. Now it was the three of us, trying to see stars through thick smoke. Maw played our ribs like a washboard. She tickled him out of us. We laughed so that there was no space for the truth. I kept the memory of us writhing around on wet grass. Even Maw couldn't kill the love of it. Brighter and bolder than anything we heard through thin plywood walls. I hope the memory stuck to him like it did to me. Without it, I don't know what we had.

When he broke his six days of silence, Jamie talked too much. He said things no one wanted to hear. It felt like he was betraying Maw and what that night in the yard stood for. I wondered why he would do anything to spoil it. She hid the radio and bent the antennas on our TV set. For months, we could only play to where the gravel ended and the asphalt began. When he came back from aunt Sarah's, there was no middle to him. Sarah tried her best to provide a semblance of home. She showed him how to mend the wings of small birds, how to dig up and dry roots for tea. But all children need to crouch in their secret nests. Vern and Maw spent their time trying to keep him from run-ning. Ma'd lock us in our room but Jamie couldn't be kept inside. He'd climb out the window and sleepwalk back into the wild. I pretended not to hear it happening. Turned as the window opened and he fell through onto a pile of mud and leaves. I was afraid of him. I wished I had his courage. We were told to play in the light because the devil was rubbing himself raw. It was in this space that the Bald-Knob grew wild.

As we got a little older, he never stopped talking about the Howlers like they were real. Jamie kept believing; he believed they were out there and said he wanted to show me them. We waited until Maw had had enough booze to keep her lean. Until Vern's truck pulled out and the sun crawled back into its shell. Just enough light in the air to still see everything in blue outline.

'Come see,' he said, as he pulled me out the window. 'They're out there.' My limbs shook as he told me where to put my feet, told me what to hang onto so that I wouldn't plummet like a fledgling. He held my hand and we ran across the yard, shushing the dog. Her muzzle lifted; she was mine. He dug a small rut and we crawled through a gap under the fence. He wanted to share this with me, because it was his to share. His way of coping. The pines were so close you could smell them. We pushed through as the last light melted. You could see any-thing in there if you went deep enough, anything at all. I held onto my bandages as branches got caught and tried to rip off the mummy-hel-met. My nose ran wild. Jamie kept pulling, further and further into the undergrowth like he'd done it a thousand times with his eyes closed. Like there was something bigger that was pulling us along.

Our breaths small against the universe, close, and so many movements in the branches above. So much unseen—eyes, eyes, eyes—and us running. We reached a small clearing. Water by my naked feet, the earth smelled wet. Jamie was out of breath. I could feel him staring at me waiting for a reaction. We were surrounded by tall trees and the sounds behind them. I knew this place. We were back there. Back where it began.

'We need to holler,' he said to me and took a step back puffing up his chest. I had never screamed in my life. I had never used my voice. So, I stood there in the fading light not knowing what my broth-er wanted of me, not quite seeing.

'Why're we out here, dummy?' is all I managed and felt him shudder.

'You need to see them, like I seen them,' he said and started screaming. Howling up into the hole of the sky. He pounded hard on his tiny chest. I felt the rawness in his throat and the silence that came when he gathered for breath. My face tingled. He jumped into the creek kicking up water as he screamed. I just watched him do it, I watched through my one good eye and felt the Bald-Knob pushing his beak into the deepest parts. Jamie's voice grew hoarse and pained but he wouldn't stop hollering into the night.

'Where are you?' he said 'You sons of bitches.' He was so alone out here. Channeling the thing we all had deep down inside us. Jamie's cry was the cry of all us pathetic creatures, all us ignored souls. As I held onto my bandages, my eye wept pus, and it started happening. I felt a warmth rising from gut to my mouth. It wasn't my heart. Sound came, new and clear. I heard my voice for the first time, born into my brother's arms, his wild dancing shape. It leapt from me like some great cougar, a panther, a painter that prowled around us and sharpened its claws on the bark. Jamie's smile fell over my body. We shared this magic blood. This new scream replaced the terror of the accident. We did it for us, for Ma, and for Wilf Batty. It was new, bold, and brave and, for a moment, I felt fearless. Jamie ran over, grabbed my shoulders, and pulled me into the shallow stream that ran through the woods. We were both water dancers on the brink of everything.

I let go of the bandages. They rippled into the water and were gone, washed away. I let go and we undressed, tearing off our shorts and tops and let the water carry them away too, let them soak forever. It was just our skins kissed by the night. We danced and screamed and played with each other's bodies, like we always did when we were bored and no one was watching. We rubbed and wriggled falling down in ecstasy. The Bald-Knob let me go, he let me go and I was a boy again. I was Blake. Jamie pushed him out and drew me in as our voices, our gleeful screams built and built upward. There were no faces staring back at me. There were no black cats exploding. It was me and him, it was us.

'Can you see 'em yet?' he said heaving, sitting down cross-legged in the stream, his desperate eyes darting. 'They're all around. More and more. In the trees.' And he yelled and beat his chest until it sounded hollow. If I wanted to, I could see them. If I dissolved into our crooked little myth and let myself become one with it, it would all be there looking back at me in that place where man and beast mate for life. If I wanted to see them, they'd be there—the Howlers. I knew that they had to exist for Jamie, he had to think they were out there watching him, plucking him from his bed every night. And even though I felt alive, reborn and turned over like a stone; it was still for him that I saw them. I squealed in alarm. Screeched, pointing into the blackness; at what I made myself see. Huge shaggy shadows, all shoulders and man hands, deep-embedded eyes drawn into the skull, splintered embers. Their bulk weighed down the branches so that it was them that made the pines creek and not the wind.

Seeing me do this. Jamie stopped and watched. He watched as I reacted to what he told me was there. Naked, crystalline water dripping from every limb. The gaping hole to our backs that had our shorts, tops and skins. He and I both knew that we'd be walking back naked, that he'd get a beating for it. But that moment, right there in the middle of nowhere, was the center of the world, it was so much bigger than a beating. We were together in this; he saw that I saw it with him.

It was us out there.

I know it was just us.

We were the Howlers.

We were the gods, then.

Made in the USA
Middletown, DE
30 January 2024

48646759R00129